Circles a Clover

Circles a Clover

Michael Egan

Published in the UK by Everything with Words Limited
Fifth Floor, 30–31 Furnival Street ,London, EC4A 1JQ

www.everythingwithwords.com

Text copyright © Michael Egan 2021
Cover © Holly Ovenden 2021

Michael Egan has asserted his right under the Copyright, Design
and Patents Act 1988 to be identified as the author of this work.

A CIP catalogue record for this book is available
from the British Library.

ISBN: 978-1-911427-20-9

Printed and bound in Great Britain by
CPI Group (UK) Ltd, Croydon CRO 4YY

On the day the world ends
A bee circles a clover,
A fisherman mends a glimmering net.

A Song on the End of the World
by Czesław Miłosz

for Seren

Chapter One

Far away, beyond the confines of her life, there was a war.

Or there wasn't a war because war was only ever really a war when you knew someone who had been hurt in it, really knew them, not just read about them on *Humans of New York* or saw them in a wheelchair on the train to Liverpool.

Or the war was just a black flag, now risen, soon falling, soon rising.

Or maybe war, all of war, was just a story someone needed to tell because the world turns like that, story upon story, one ends and another begins, a voice speaks, the world listens.

Or there wasn't a war at all, there were only bad choices like there have always been bad choices and the regrets of men with too much power so their tiny mistakes, their small catastrophes, were like great hammers being brought down on brittle shells. Everyone was just a brittle shell.

Or, once unshackled, even islands might be cast adrift and when the sea-storms woke there would be little to save that land from drowning; lonely, submerged to nothing, arm outstretched in search of fingers that were too far away to grip and anyway refused to grip.

Or, the worst truth to know, there was a war and it was creeping closer, stealthily, inevitably, ready to break down the walls of her world at some too-close, too-soon point in her future. No hammer, just light. Just thunder in the night.

That was what her dad had been saying for months. He knew beyond a doubt that the world was about to end. She could never believe that. The world seemed the same as always. There had been angry seasons in her life already, like the wild waking to life of spring or the choking bombardments of summer's unending heat, the fallen and settling dead leaves of autumn, cast away, trodden through by west-walking feet. Now there was only winter and the bitter morning air. Wherever the war was, it wasn't happening here and though she caught glimpses on the news of upturned boats, kneeling figures, small mushroom clouds expanding in the

night as one lonely balcony shook, the ruins of ruins,
quiet bodies as if sleeping on a beach and broken
cities like the crumbled remains of a half- imagined
place, she didn't truly believe in it all. That was it;
it was like a fantasy. Like *Game of Thrones*, like how
last year on Tuesday in PE all anyone wanted to do
was talk about *Game of Thrones*. Like half the world
away was another world and that was enough distance
to make it so unreal it could never touch hers, never
touch this place. It wasn't like she didn't care. She
knew that she should care, had even cared too much
about things like that when she was little, so much so
that her dad used to turn off the news if she was in the
room but she could still listen, pretend to be playing,
while the adults talked about Iraq and she wondered
what Iraq meant and why it sounded so harsh and
metallic in her mind. And when they talked about
Afghanistan she would look up at the painting that
used to hang above the fireplace. A woman and an
Afghan hound. She used to think the woman was
her mum even though her mum had red hair and
the woman looked like she was from another place,
Afghan maybe, though she wasn't sure what Afghans
looked like.

No, she wasn't dead-hearted like some of the
others in her class who couldn't even say a thing
about the world let alone care about what was

happening as nearby as Manchester to even try to imagine what was happening over the sea, over the wide world, over the breaking. She knew what was happening, she cared, she told herself that even when her dad kept going on and on or was sat for hours on his computer, looking for the proof to what she knew was all only in his head.

She was Kyle Halfpenny and that was one certainty. She knew who she was. She knew she cared just as well as she knew her own name, that caring also a certainty. It was a truth she could never question. But she would, at times, doubt that truth until it became weak. Yes, she cared when they showed a film in school of refugees or what was left of a bomb-ruined town or when Bordeaux was attacked. But even that, Bordeaux, seemed far away. Distant, because the shouts for help were all shouted in French and the news report over-dubbed. She cried when Miss Martindale told them about gas attacks and showed them a film of children gasping for air, sweating, shaking, still burning all over and inside. Everyone had cried in class then, but even that was just a film and as far away. Everything seemed so unreal and not here. No matter what her dad said about Russian jets over the North Sea and submarines in the Baltic, wherever the Baltic was, or how Belarus was just a test or how the world was running out of chances to be a good place. She didn't believe it, not like it was something that she could touch or see happening right there in front of her eyes like when she saw Kerry Deane run into a concrete post and heard the crack of skull on stone, saw the blood trickle so slowly down the side of Kerry's face like a trickle of melting ice cream. Not like that.

There *was* a war then but it was too far away to trouble her. Almost dreamy, hazy. A nightmare, not a good dream, but one that she knew wouldn't come every night and would, anyway, go away just like bad dreams eventually did, just like everything in the news seemed to go away, to come and go, the fear and the hope, the sudden tragedy and lasting calm. The world just ebbing and shifting.

Here, now, in this place which was her place, there was no war. Just morning, how winter brings darkness into the day and makes the world seem not yet woken when it should have woken hours ago. Just winter and the difficulty of fastening her duffel's last button with half-awake fingers, pulling the fur-lined hood close about her face then drinking the last of the tepid tea and going out into the morning. Her dad was still sleeping, had left the television on all night again and his notebooks all strewn about the table. There were empty cans of San Miguel too and he'd been smoking in the garden. She knew that because the outside light was on, a moth still buzzing about it in the morning gloom.

She closed the door quietly. Out, into a day that wasn't even real yet, still night really, still yesterday really. She was always a little scared going out so early when there was hardly any light, few cars, barely anyone around. This time of day was just before the real day started, not early enough for the world to be completely asleep but not yet stretching its arms and blinking its eyes. Soon, in less than an hour, the streets would fill with cars and buses, block and slow. The children would go this way and that, some over the bridge to the private school, some out of the town towards the rough school, most her way. She locked the door quickly and glanced around their cul-de-sac before she even thought of heading over the front garden. It was silly; she wasn't even sure what she was afraid of. Someone jumping out? A crazy person just waiting for her on the off-chance she was leaving for school a little earlier than usual? But there was just quiet, just nothing. She let her school shoes crunch their way across the ice-brittle grass and almost slipped on the pavement, her feet unprepared for the black ice it hid, steadying herself on their car, the bonnet as cold as she felt within. She stayed still for a moment, balanced herself, adjusted her bag and breathed out so she could see her own breath, fog against the all-around cold. There was a light on in the bathroom of their neighbour's house and she could see the misty silhouette of a man shaving, topless. She watched him for a moment, his arm lifting slowly, the blade scraping his face, then the arm dropping out of sight, the water cleaning the blade then repeat.

She walked slowly, now rightly mistrusting the ground beneath her feet. Soon her face was freezing but her body, beneath her thick coat and wool tights, was warm. At the end of their road she sneezed and startled a rabbit that had been sat on the roundabout, sending it running fast into a garden. Suddenly more rabbits ran for cover from all along the road and she wondered if they even knew what a sneeze was. It was just a sound to them, just danger. She looked up. There were buzzards sometimes out over their back garden but none today.

A bus rolled past, a few passengers on board, all huddled against the windows, half- asleep, half-reading the *Metro*. She waited for it to pass and when it was gone she crossed, her hand going into her pocket for her cigarettes. As her fingers touched the lining of her pocket she remembered they were on her windowsill, with her lighter and her *Breaking Bad* mug, the mug full of ash-tainted milk and butts losing their tan-paper covering. She ground her teeth, a habit she hadn't shifted since she was little, ran her tongue over her front teeth and walked faster. There was no wind but the air was sharp with ice and soon her face was warming, her cheeks reddening with her quickening pace. Cerys and Hannah would be in a little early too, she remembered; maybe they would have cigarettes and they could sneak down by the woods for one before they went in. Why had she even decided to go in so ridiculously early, the question nagged as she almost slipped again as she passed the private school? It wasn't like she needed to go to the library and get some extra revision done or finish her coursework or that she was so desperate to see anyone. She steadied herself, too aware now of the ice beneath her shoes. It was her dad, she knew that. Every other morning he would be up with her no matter how much he had drank the night before, telling her all his crazy thoughts, telling her how they needed to go away and showing her the reports he had cut from newspapers or copied word-for-word from some cookie-virused website. Better to pretend to need to revise than suffer that. Sometimes she thought that maybe she was sort of doing him a favour by not giving him an audience, like if he didn't have anyone to tell all that stuff he would just stop thinking about it, shut up and get better, maybe even go back to work. She let her hand trail along the frozen branches of a bare hedge beside the nursery. It had been her nursery once. She stopped and looked through the mesh fence into a world she sort of remembered, vaguely. She saw the swings and slide and couldn't remember for certain if they had been there, the same ones, when she was there. She saw the milk bottles left outside the locked gate and remembered how some mornings the teacher would show the milk bottle with a hole right through the gold top and tell them about naughty magpies and they would all make yukky sounds when the teacher took a big gulp of the milk and told them now she might turn into a magpie. *Do you have anything shiny, Harry?* the teacher would say and Harry would squirm away as she tiptoed closer. *Who's got something shiny, how about you Jonah, what about you Lilly, come on, one of you must have something shiny?* And she would come to Kyle last. *I know you have something shiny, Kyle.* The teacher would tiptoe closer. Even though she knew it was a joke, still Kyle would gasp and hide her mother's necklace down her dress.

"I haven't," Kyle would say. "I haven't got anything shiny, anything."

She frowned. No, she didn't think the swings and slides had been there then. There had only been a little square of wood chippings where they would play zombies.

Memories, she hated how once one tumbled out others came with it. She could see her mum picking her up, at that door, just like it was happening now, today. She hated that. It wasn't fair.

She took out her phone and skimmed through her call history for the unnamed number. As the phone rang she watched the nursery door, still white, still pictures painted by the children stuck to the glass, still the same when nothing else was. She knew no one would answer because that was something that never changed. Every time she rang the number she half expected the line to just go dead and a robot voice tell her the number was no longer available, or worse, someone to actually answer and tell her, no, they have always had this number and no, they knew no one by that name. She ended the call. She wasn't sure which was worse, probably the dead line, maybe the stranger's voice.

She crossed at the village's hart signpost, the deer white as snow against black and it was there she saw the fox.

There were lights on in the vets and even though the lights shone right onto it, lighting it up, the fox sat in the road licking its paw as if the world didn't matter.

She stopped, took out her phone. It licked one paw and then the next and then it stood on all fours and stretched its back. She zoomed in, took a few pictures, careful not to make too much noise, but even as she took them she wondered if the fox would really care. *Surely foxes care less about danger than rabbits.* No buzzards to swoop, no sneeze to startle. She scanned through the images, deleted a badly focused shot and chose the best. In it the fox was looking off down the road, backlit by the light from the vets, head high, tail low. She uploaded it to her Instagram and when she was done the fox was still there.

"If you stay there all day I won't be able to cross," she said, whispered.

The fox turned its head towards her as if he heard her. Understood her. The rumble of an engine grew closer. A car was coming down the road from the direction of town but still he didn't move. He looked at her, grey-black eyes holding her gaze, unfazed.

She could see the headlights of the car, close. She clapped her hands in an attempt to scare the fox but still he stood there, watching her, his back now bowed a little and tail raised, almost challenging her.

"Go away!" she shouted, clapping her cold hands harder, wishing she'd put her gloves on no matter there was a hole in a palm. "Come on, go!"

The car was near. Why wouldn't the fox move? She waved an arm, clapped. It seemed like he would

11

never move, just let the car hit him, run him down, end him. But at last the fox looked right, looked down the road towards the approaching car and calmly turned away from any danger before running towards the garden of the vets, gone.

When the car had passed, she kept walking. Water touched her face and looking up she saw a light snow was falling, faint flakes melting even before they reached the heat of her body, at the suggestion of her.

By the time she reached school the snow was much heavier, as heavy as it had been yesterday when it hadn't settled, even though the view outside of French was one of utter whiteness. There was a boy from her class, Spencer Munroe, leaning against the gate, smoking like he didn't care if a teacher saw him. He didn't. There were other Year 11s in early too, all milling about.

"Do you want one?" asked Spencer as she passed him.

He was frowning, like he was puzzled, like he was trying to guess her answer. "I don't smoke," she said, she lied. "Not much anyway."

He nodded and leaned back against the gate, half-closed his eyes as he took a drag. She took a breath of the snowy air instead and hurried on to the main entrance where

Cerys was waiting, not wanting to go in alone even though it was freezing. Cerys was running her hand over her thick fringe, straightening it. Her hair was curly, falling down past her shoulders but her fringe was precisely trimmed, straight.

"Did you speak to Spencer?" gasped Cerys, looking past Kyle to the gate.

Kyle looked back as the snow settled on her hood and coat. There was something of Spencer that was like the fox, stood there at the gate, still, unbothered by the world, unmoved by danger. Not a bit like her dad, not a bit like her really. The snow fell heavier so that she knew it would settle. Cerys pushed the double doors open and quickly, before any more snow could fall upon them, the two entered the warmth of school.

Chapter Two

The world outside was a consistent white land and still the snow didn't cease, heavier and heavier it fell, on and on.

Her table was near the window and as she sat, her fingers tracing a circle on the table's top, she tried to ignore the chatter around her of her classmates as they waited for Miss Pepperdine to appear and start afternoon registration. She had hardly eaten anything at lunch, just some chips and yoghurt, and even though she hadn't felt a bit hungry then, now her stomach felt empty of anything. She watched the snow falling. It seemed slow, laboured, like there was so much of it, so close together, that it was struggling even to fall, buffering like a dodgy download. Below the classroom window there was a fence that separated the school grounds from the woods. There was a path close to the fence that led through the woods all the way along the canal and eventually into town. She could see a man with a low- pulled wool hat on, a chocolate Labrador walking reluctantly at his side, before both disappeared into the thicker trees.

Kyle had walked through the woods at least once a week since she was little. Back then it was with her dad and Skan, their dog Torres too. Now it was with Cerys and the others after school if it was a nice day, a slower walk into town where they would get a Costa and take their time going home, talking about what boy Cerys was messaging and what boys Kyle would message if she ever got their numbers.

"All you do is ask," Cerys would tell her but Kyle doubted it was that easy. "But if they say no, I've asked haven't I? They'll know why I asked."

Cerys would turn her mocha around; she hardly ever drank them. Just turned the oversized mug around on the table so some of the chocolatey liquid would spill and a ring would form on the table beneath it. "Yeah, because you like them."

"Exactly. That's what makes it horrible."

"You don't have to be so scared of someone knowing you like them, Kyle," Hannah would say.

It's not that easy to not be scared. She never said the words.

She never used to be so scared to do things. Take the woods. When she was little, running through with Skan ahead of her, chasing him or him chasing her. Not even slowing to cross the old rickety bridges that spanned river-dry little valleys beneath, to dodge the dog muck and the low wastewater pipe that was so out of place, just before the last and longest bridge. She wasn't scared of falling or tripping or whacking her head then. All she cared about was running with Skan and laughing and who could reach the water first even when their dad was shouting behind them to slow down and Torres was barking madly at a heron.

The wind picked up so the snow was being blown sideways, slowly, reluctantly. Miss. Pepperdine still wasn't there and in awareness of her absence the noise of the others was getting louder. She looked to the door. Some other teacher on the corridor, Mr Greasedale probably, would come in roaring for quiet soon if they kept it up. She looked back to the woods.

Skan had taken her there the day before he left. It was summer, so hot that the old woman three houses down had been taken to hospital in an ambulance that morning. So hot that as they walked she wondered if there was any air left, it hurt so much to breathe. They had walked slowly, taking their time.

Torres had been left at home because their dad had said the dog wasn't to go in the woods anymore.

"I swear it was a wolf," he had said, banging a cupboard door like he had started to back then, angry at everything and anything. "Came out of nowhere and leapt on Torres. Course Torres fought back, what else would he do? Poor bugger had no chance. I had to drag the thing off him and this woman, girl really, she runs over all apologetic but you could tell she couldn't control the bloody beast. Tell you what, they shouldn't let them off their leads if they can't control them."

So it had just been her and Skan, Iskander, because her dad loved to read about Alexander the Great and anything like that, Mesopotamia and Macedonia, the long past. Skan always told her that she had been lucky.

"If Mum hadn't put her foot down," he told her once while they ate fish fingers and waffles and watched *Home and Away*, "Dad would've called you Scheherazade."

He was sixteen then, just finished Year 11. He had messed up every last exam though her dad didn't have a clue, not yet. She was eleven, not yet started at the high school. When they reached the canal they sat on the jetty and took off their shoes and socks and dangled their feet in the water. Even the water

18

was warm but it was some small relief against the heat. Water boatmen raced over the calm surface, a kingfisher darted out of the reeds and then was gone. There were moorhens, there were always moorhens. There was a red flower, not a rose just a flower, growing by the water and she remembered when she was five and Skan told her there were trolls all about the woods, that the fallen trees were really sleeping trolls. Once, a little cruelly, he had run off and left her alone.

"The trolls are coming!" he had screamed before racing away, leaving her there, terrified, alone. "They're coming for your blood, Kyle," he had called from some hidden place.

She had tried to run after him but her legs were only little and there was a noise. She swore it was a growl or grunt and there, right in a mess of fallen branches, like something had just trampled down through the trees, breaking branch after branch on their way down, was something red. She hadn't stayed to find out what. She ran, screaming and then Skan was there. He'd been sorry, really sorry, and hugged her close telling her he'd never leave her, not for real.

But with their feet in the warm water of the canal he had told he *was* leaving. "Where will you go?" she had asked, trying not to cry.

He put an arm around her, his skin sweaty against her own sticky neck. He shrugged. "Liverpool maybe," he said. "Skeebo's brother went to London last year and he's working in a bar now, got a flat."

They were quiet. The moorhens swam around but there were no ducks, just the black moorhens with their blood-red beaks.

"Why do you have to go anywhere though?" she said at last, not trying to hold back crying now. "It's not fair. What's wrong with here? You can't just leave me, I'm here."

He pulled his arm away and huffed.

"Come on, Kyle. You know I have to, I can't put up with Dad and all his crap anymore. I've had enough, that's all."

Her lips wouldn't stop quivering, the tears really flowing no matter she didn't want them to. "What about me? You won't come back, you know you won't."

Skan took a cigarette out and lit it. The smoke smelled woody to her, not like the roll- ups her dad smoked that smelled rough and made her cough.

"I can't stay, you know I can't."

She rubbed her eyes, willed the tears to stop but they wouldn't. "Do you think Mum left because she'd had enough?"

Skan smoked and kicked his feet. He never liked

talking about their mum. She got why. He was older when she left; Kyle had only been a baby really. Skan had been in the hall watching her go, their dad screaming at her he said though he never told Kyle what their dad was screaming.

"Anyway, you can visit when you're older. You've never been to London, I haven't even. Skeebo says there's nowhere like it. His little brother came to visit and he took him to the Natural History Museum. You like dinosaurs, right?"

She nodded. It wasn't really true. She had liked dinosaurs for a while when she was seven, just a little while. She'd already googled the Natural History Museum, seen the brontosaurus. It had scared her a little because it wasn't a real dinosaur. It was just bones, all the skin and realness stripped away, just bare bones. She didn't like that, didn't like that the dinosaurs were from long ago and now there were none left. Now dinosaurs were just birds, just kingfishers skimming still water.

"There you go then, we can go there and there's loads more to do. Skeebo says you could walk round London for a week and not get bored, not even come close to seeing all of it. It's a proper place, Kyle. Not like here. Least there won't be any trolls there."

"Blood trolls," she said, not looking at him.

21

"Yeah, no blood trolls. None at all. Just cockney goblins maybe, something like that." His laugh was small and unsure. He flicked his cigarette, half-smoked, into the water. "Don't worry, I'll talk to Dad before I go. I'll tell him he has to get help, you know like the tablets he used to take, see the doctor or whatever." His arm went round her again and she nestled into it. "Anyway, you've always been his favourite. You two, you're the same really except you're not mad. Well, not yet."

He pinched her ear and she laughed.

"I promise I'll always call and stuff," he said, standing. "I'd never just abandon you, not like…"

He didn't finish that sentence but she knew what he wanted to say.

She kept her feet in the water. *Maybe if I just stay here with my feet in the water, so that I can't walk anywhere, just stay right here, he won't go.*

But Skan had put his hand out and she had let him lift her up. Along the path he picked a flower for her, not a red one, just a wildflower like the ones that grew all over the woods. He pushed the stem into her hair and kissed her on her forehead. They walked all the way to town even though the day grew hotter. At the lock they rested and watched it fill. There was a middle class-looking couple on a canal boat, both with the same designer glasses and matching lemon polo shirts. They looked like teachers, thought Kyle, as the water rushed in from one lock to another, the boat rising and rising.

She turned away from the window. There was a display of poems on the wall across from her. Year 7 poems. The display was decorated with drawings of Frankenstein's monster and Dracula, a haunted house and a ghost with a round booing mouth. That was the first thing Miss Pepperdine got all her new Year Sevens to do, write a poem to scare someone. Think of the scariest thing you can, make it really frightening, use scary adjectives like monstrous and bloodthirsty and deathly. Kyle had written one about trolls, blood trolls. Jay Morosini said that no one had ever heard of blood trolls, that it was a stupid poem and not even scary, but Miss Pepperdine had let her draw the troll and Kyle had drawn it standing in a field of red flowers. She told everyone that the flowers were blood flowers.

"You have quite a dark mind don't you, Kyle?" Miss Pepperdine had said as she collected the poems and drawings in.

That night she rang Skan to read him her poem but there was no answer. It was like that for the next few months, no answer or just a text back to say he was busy working and then eventually he stopped answering all together and she gave up texting. That Christmas he sent a card to her telling her he was sorry but he had to find his own life, he couldn't always be there whenever she needed just to speak to him, that she had to start looking after herself like he had always had to. Memories, she hated them.

Chris Hardaker and Jack Crane were on the table behind her.

"I wouldn't want there to be zombies," Chris was saying. "That'd be rubbish, having to run all the time and when you finally find somewhere safe, something crap happens and you're running again. No way."

Jack had a *Doctor Who* pencil case, he'd had it since Year Seven. "Yeah but you could fight zombies at least. Look at *The Walking Dead*, there's loads of characters in that who wouldn't stand a chance against aliens or something and they're alright, they survive."

"That's TV," said Chris. "It's not like in films where everyone has to be hero. In TV you don't have to be like a proper hero, you can be shit and get away with it for a bit."

Jack saw Kyle watching them. He was chubby and there was too much wax in his hair and he looked at her too often for too long. " How would you want the world to end, Kyle?"

24

Chris was looking at her too. She didn't mind Chris, he was tall and played basketball even though he was friends with Jack.

"What?" she said. "What do you mean?"

Chris leaned forward. He had braces but that wasn't too bad a thing. By sixth form Cerys would probably be messaging him.

"Like what apocalypse would you prefer?" he said, smiling nervously. "Zombies?

Aliens? Super flu?"

She was about to tell him she didn't have any idea how the world might end and didn't want to have any idea, when the chatter around them quietened.

Miss. Pepperdine came in first. Kyle looked at the clock: there were only ten minutes of form left and her stomach still felt hollow. Behind Miss Pepperdine came Mr Finnegan, the head, and behind him came the RE teacher, Mrs Shah. It was Mrs Shah who always gave the talks in assembly on sex and Snapchat and how to avoid being groomed by old men or terrorists even though Kyle was pretty sure her school was the least likely place for any of that. All three of them looked serious, as heavy with it as the snow outside. That drained the atmosphere right away. Everyone sat forward, quiet and waiting. Something had obviously happened, someone had obviously done something. Maybe someone had been caught smoking pot by the garage or Carl Chapman had been taking pictures of Year Nine girls again.

Miss Pepperdine didn't speak. It was Mr Finnegan who told them.

"Last night there was a car accident..." he began. When he said Rose's name, Hannah screamed and Sachana Groves fell from her chair so that Mrs Shah had to run over and help her stand, though Sachana wouldn't move; she just sat on the floor, crying, sobbing, her body limp.

Kyle knew she should have been more upset by the news than she was. She hadn't even noticed Rose wasn't in. When the other girls started crying she knew she should cry too but she couldn't. Not a single tear or even the hint of a tear. That was okay, she told herself, to be dumbstruck, to be shocked. Maybe that's what everyone would think, that she was so shocked by the news, as crushed as everyone else.

When Mr Finnegan left and Mrs Shah had told them there would be counselling for all Year 11s who needed it Period Five, Miss Pepperdine sat on her table and for the first time, Kyle could see she had been crying, her dark eyeshadow washed away.

The girls kept crying, Cerys and Lara, Hannah and Bethan, even Stacey Unsworth who absolutely hated Rose and who Rose hated back just as much. They were crying and couldn't stop. A couple of the boys were crying too, their heads on their desks, hiding their faces. Yes, Rose had been her friend, not a friend who she would message every night or even go for a Costa in town with, but a friend she had known since nursery, years and years. A life. But even though she knew she should be crying, even though she could feel the sadness right down deep inside her, a hard ball that wanted to let go, explode, she sat there, watching the snow fall slower and slower, as if time itself was slowing, reversing until eventually it might stop all together. Though she knew that could never happen.

Chapter Three

It was Ismail Kenny who got the cider and Kane Richards was the one who got the vodka because their uncle ran the *Bargain Booze* and didn't care that much anyway about you being 18 or not.

Unorganised, twelve of them walked down to the Blue Bridge and found a sheltered place away from the path. There was a fence, low and weak, but the boys leaned on it anyway and the girls huddled together beneath the bridge and passed the vodka back and forth. At first they didn't really speak. It was snowing still and the cold had only grown, harsher, deeper, yet no one made any move to go home. Sachana was crying, hadn't stopped hardly since they'd left school and Cerys was hugging her, one shoulder of her coat wet with Sachana's tears. Spencer was there too, sitting in the snow so his trousers must have been soaked but he didn't seem worried by that. He held a cigarette in his hand, not smoking it, listening to Ismail telling them all what his brother said really happened. How Rose was with some older college boy from Winsford way, someone said his name was Nathan.

"He was ragging his Mini down past Kelsall, along the bypass," Ismail told them in his thick Manchester accent. "Just fucking spun out, hit a wall. Mo reckons Rose was the only one really hurt, I mean killed or whatever, even though there were three others in the back."

"Who else was in the back?" asked Kane.

Ismail swigged the cider straight from the bottle. "Fucked if I know, his mates I think. Not from up here."

They were silent for a while then, passing the bottles around, smoking. Abby told a story about the dance exam last year. Kyle didn't do dance but she had gone to the show that year and they were right, Rose was a dancer, like she could have been a really good dancer if she'd trained and kept training. If she hadn't died.

"What about Fern?" said Cerys suddenly. Fern was Rose's little sister, a Year Ten. "What about her?" someone said.

"Has anyone messaged her?"

30

No one had. They drank. The snow finally stopped but it seemed to get even colder and darker. A couple walked by, quickly when they saw the huddle. Ismail shook the half- empty vodka bottle at them so the taller woman scowled at him defiantly but didn't slow her pace.

Kyle tried to remember something solid, real, about Rose but everything was old. Like how she could just remember that when they were in nursery their mums would pick them up early one day a week, on Wednesday, and they would always be there at the door together, waiting for noon. That was one of the only memories she had of her mum that was real, not made up like some of the other ones: a true memory. Or how when they went into high school they were sat in the scary hall and for some reason they held hands as they were given their forms and how happy they were when they were both put in Kolbe even though they knew they weren't friends, not truly.

"I think we should do something for her," said Cerys, shivering. Kane passed the cider to Spencer. "What, like a tribute?"

A few nodded.

"Isn't it too soon for that?" said Kyle. She hadn't drunk a drop, not like the others. She'd just smoked, one after another like cigarettes were running out forever.

"It's too soon for everything," said Spencer, still sat in the snow, half looking at her, half looking past her.

"She deserves something," said Cerys timidly, playing with her fringe again.

Ross Copp had a stone in his hand and he threw it hard towards the canal but there was no sound of it hitting the water. "Like some idiot not driving her into a wall."

That and the snow returning ended the night. When the few of them who lived in the village were near The Red Lion, Spencer started walking next to her. He had his cigarettes out.

"You do smoke," he said, handing her one.

She didn't argue. Lit it and kept pace with him though he walked hard and the snow's cold was burning her face. Her nose must have been bright red, she realised as she lit the cigarette.

"I just didn't want one then."

They were walking into the snow now. It was strange, the snow. She couldn't remember a day when it had snowed so much, stayed so deep and everywhere. As she walked she pushed her shoes against it, pushed a trough through it.

"Did you like her?" said Spencer. He had his phone in one hand, tapping the screen. "I think I used to. I mean I don't think I disliked her."

He nodded, still tapping and walking. "Same. I

mean I kissed her and stuff last year but I don't think kissing someone means you really like them does it?"

Ismail, Cerys, Sachana and Louise Johns were behind them, their voices lost because she didn't want to hear them; let the wind muffle them.

"I don't think so," she said.

"Me neither." He put his phone away. They were passing the graveyard; a broken umbrella leaned against the bus shelter, its parts jutting out towards the pavement, metal arms reaching out to scrape at passers-by.

"Do you know you're meant to hold your breath when you pass a graveyard," Spencer said.

She'd never heard of that. "Who said so?"

Ismail had caught up with them, grinning, a little too drunk. "I've heard that, it's so the dead can't steal your soul from you, your breath. We should do it, you know, just in case."

All of them did it, took deep breaths. Kyle glanced back, saw Sachana and Cerys linking arms, mouths tight shut, holding their breaths, all of them doing the same as they hurried past the graves. That seemed odd, all of them alive and trying to keep their breath in, away from the dead, when someone they knew had no breath left. None at all. Not a drop or a gasp or whisper. She wasn't sure how breaths were measured but drop seemed the least likely. Whisper: that was

33

it, a whisper of a breath. She breathed out and like that the graves and the long-dead were behind them. Ismail and Spencer were laughing, Spencer's turning into a hard cough as the air rushed back into his lungs.

As they reached the end of Bradburns Lane he asked her which way she was going. "That way," she said, pointing left to the roundabout.

"I live up near town but I can walk you if you like."

"Come on," said Cerys as the others waited for Spencer to follow. "I'm freezing."

"If you want," she told him.

When the others were away past the Methodist church he offered her another cigarette. Her throat felt raw with smoking; it was all she could taste but still she took it and lit it, breathed in the harsh heat of it.

"What do you listen to?" he said as they passed the field where a rich family kept llamas.

She hated questions like that. Sometimes she would sit in her room and make playlists on Spotify just so she had a good answer, but the truth was she didn't listen really. She wished she did have some band she loved or some music she couldn't go a day without listening to, but she didn't.

"I just listen to whatever," she said because the

name of every band she had ever listened to had left her, gone.

He frowned, disappointed, fastened the top button of his coat and tucked his chin into it against the cold. "Me too I suppose, except I think I listen to some songs too much. Sometimes I listen to one song so much I kind of start thinking it's mine, like it's just for me. You ever do that?"

She laughed. "No, I don't think I have."

They were getting near her house. She slowed her pace, trying her best to slow Spencer's with it. He seemed to walk in a rush all the time, hardly powering on but still like he was trying to get somewhere all the time except when he stopped. When he wasn't walking, he seemed as static and calm as anyone she had ever known. To her relief as she slowed he fell in with her as they followed the curved wall, snow-heavy trees above them, the llamas inside their huts at the back of the field.

"Did you know I was in a band?" he said. He wasn't bragging, she could hear that in his voice. It was just a statement, not a boast. "I'm not great, not good even. But I think we're good together, like it doesn't matter how shit I am because the others are better."

She could see the streetlight at the end of her road, a marker to end their walk when she didn't want it to end, even though it was just a walk. She'd hardly

looked at him, just nodded and walked too slowly,
smoked too slowly.

"What do you play?"

He shrugged again. "Sort of indie I suppose. I like
old American punk though, do you?"

She'd never listened to any punk, any at all. "I
think so."

He moved his head a little like he was listening to
a song. Or maybe it was just the coldness of the air.
"Some days I only ever listen to the Ramones, you
know. That's just how I get. I like get stuck on some
old band, can't give them up."

Now they were under the streetlight's glow and
she could see the porch light in her house, nestled in
the middle curve of the cul-de-sac. Her house looked
warm. She wanted to go there, get in bed, sleep. But
she stopped and dropped her cigarette, barely smoked,
to the snow.

"Do you think you'll go uni?" he asked.

She looked back again at her house, wondered if
her dad was worried where she was though he hadn't
rung or messaged her. He was probably in his study
again, copying words that weren't even true, putting
all the broken pieces of nothing back together, forcing
them to make sense and fit.

She felt a sudden urgency to talk, to show him she
was just as real as he was.

"I want to but my dad wants me to stay close, Liverpool or Manchester. Miss. Meredith says I should focus on Science but I hate Science. I couldn't be a doctor or anything like that, you know thinking about what's inside us all the time or why what's inside us works and breaks. I'd hate that. I don't know, I always wanted to just be what my mum was."

"Your mum?" Spencer was close to her, his coat almost touching her coat. Even though it was freezing, the wind like waves of ice, she felt warm, as if they were in a little cocoon of their own heat. She knew why. She wondered if he felt as warm but even now when she looked at him she could hardly bear to look at his eyes. This was the part Cerys was always telling her she got wrong. *I'm too scared of what comes next.*

"She was a librarian in Chester, I mean when I was little. I don't think you need a degree for that but I always thought it would be nice to do."

He nodded, like he understood something suddenly. "You like books then?"

She thought of lying, making up for her music answer, naming some of the books her dad had on his bookshelf like *A Brief History of Seven Killings* or *The Bone Clocks*, one of the new Jo Nesbo ones Uncle Pete had sent him for his birthday. There was only one book she'd ever really liked, the one Skan said their mum read to them and Skan read to her after she had left even though it used to scare her a little. *The Eagle of the Ninth.* Truthfully, she hadn't looked at that for years, couldn't even remember if it was actually about an eagle. It was imagining the words becoming something real that always held her back. She could imagine, yes, close her eyes and see whatever awaited her within herself, the hope and worry, the fantasy and fear, but to read someone else's imaginings, to actually see what they saw within themselves as real, no, that was strange to her. It was as strange and wrong as breaking into someone's house and wearing their clothes, sleeping in their bed, kissing their child goodnight.

"Not really, not anymore. To tell the truth, I don't read anything really." He laughed. His laugh was like his cough, hard-edged, uneasy.

He brushed his hand over some branches so the snow that was caught there fell away. "You live with your dad then?"

"Just us."

"Me too. I mean just me and mum. What's that like, just you and your dad?"

She glanced back again. The porch light wasn't on anymore but the living room light was, and the curtains were open so she could see the television's flickers.

"It's okay most of the time." She never talked about her dad to anyone, not even to Cerys. That was always her world, hidden behind a wall like the llamas, a sign saying Private Property for anyone who tried to look in, for trespassers. No one needed to know how ill her dad was or how he hadn't worked for three years or how some nights he wouldn't sleep and she would hear him talking to himself though she couldn't hear the exact words or how some mornings she would come downstairs and smell burning toast and find him sat on the kitchen floor just crying or that when she found him like that she would never go to him, tell him she was there, how instead she would slip out the front door to school, close the door as quietly as possible and leave him, run to the end of their road and ring Cerys to talk about anything, anything other than that.

"He's not well," she said, not even knowing why she said it. "I mean I think he wants us to go away."

"Away?"

"Yeah, away from here, away from England altogether. He thinks the world is going to end."

Spencer laughed but when she didn't laugh with him he stopped and looked at her, eyes a little wide.

"You're serious. Shit, that's mad. Why would he think that?"

That was enough, the wall was still standing, why

push it any more. Private Property. "He's not well," she said, shrugging. "He just gets like this sometimes. Don't worry, he's not right about that stuff."

He laughed again. "You're weird aren't you?"

She could see he had a gap between his front teeth, as wide as the prong of a fork, and wondered why she'd never noticed it before. She shrugged like he shrugged.

"I wish. I'm proper boring." "Nah, I don't think you're that."

He moved a little closer to her but then his head dropped, his chin tucked deeper into his coat, his black hair flopping over his eyes.

"Don't tell anyone," he said, without looking up. "I slept with her last year."

The warmth vanished. Now there was just the wind, the snow, the chill. She wished Cerys was there to be a witness. *See, that's why it's better my way.*

"Rose," she said and he nodded.

"It was only a one-off, I was pretty drunk." "Were you seeing each other?"

"Nah, just out at the fair in Weaverham last summer and you know. Stuff happens when you've drunk a whole bottle of Tesco cider."

"It does," she lied but she didn't want him to talk anymore now. It was cold, too cold. She wanted to be home and in bed and away from everyone else's lives, all their drunk sex and Snapchats and older boys from Winsford and cars hitting walls.

He shuffled back, away from her. "You won't say will you?" "No. Why would I?"

"It was just once. She wouldn't even message me after that, just proper ignored me. Started seeing some lad from Frodsham like a week later. I don't think he was the same one with the car though, you know, *that* car."

He looked like he was about to walk away then, leave her, but instead he glanced up, through his hair, eyes narrowed like he wasn't sure about something. "Do you want to do something after school this week?"

Her face was ice. She was glad of that; at least if she was blushing he might think she was just freezing. "Like what?"

"Walk, coffee in town, whatever you want."

Cerys would have told her to kiss him, take the initiative, but she didn't. She folded her arms over her chest, a prison, barring him. No, it wasn't that. She was cold. *I'm just cold, not dead.*

She risked a smile. "Yeah."

"Okay then. Thursday?"

She nodded and he smiled back at her, the little gap showing again. "See you later then," he said.

His breath had form; the cold had given it some

41

life. Like smoke, it reached out of him when he spoke, towards her. *You can kiss me now.*

"Yeah, bye," she said.

He pulled up his hood and walked out into the slurry-troughed road, ridged furrows of grey made by what little slow-moving traffic had ventured out. Halfway across he stopped, took out a cigarette. She watched him as his ice-locked fingers tried to flick his lighter awake but time and again the flame wouldn't catch. A car was nearing, slow, careful. Spencer didn't move, just kept trying to light the cigarette stubbornly. The car was moving too slowly for her to be scared he might be hit, but still she wanted to call out to him to be careful but that would only have told him she was watching him. *You're a weirdo aren't you?* She stayed silent and eventually she saw the faintest little light of fire joining to the cigarette and as he sucked on it the cigarette caught the fire and he walked on.

The gate creaked as she pushed it open, the latch still not fixed. In the front garden everything was white: the bare rosebushes and the hedge and the gnomes. All white. The little pewter statue of a girl with a bird perched on her hand that her father had dug up out of the back garden when he was clearing space for the new shed was the only thing not completely covered. Half-submerged, its silly bonnet and curly hair poked out of the snow, its smiling face ridiculously happy. The statue was stuck and unable to make itself free almost like it had given in to being slowly covered.

She could hear music as she opened the front door. It was on low, one of her dad's favourites. *Wichita Lineman*. She hated that song. He used to sing it to her when she was little even though he had an awful singing voice, but she hated the song, not his out-of-tune voice. It was like a funeral song, too sad, too full of the weight of a stranger's bad memories.

"Dad," she called but he didn't answer. She could smell some kind of dinner congealing in the oven, trapped between two plates, mash and sausage and beans and gravy all merging into one mouth-burning gloop.

The living room light was the only light on in the whole house. She dropped her school bag onto the couch and took off her coat, let the deep heat of the central heating find a way into her icy bones. He wasn't in the living room but the television was on as always, the sound off, Jeremy Paxman mouthing questions and posh students silently mouthing their answers back.

"Dad," she called again.

There were two suitcases propped up against the

other couch, both shut. She went over to them, lifted one for the weight and felt it was heavy.

"Dad!" she shouted, more desperate. On the table was a bottle of Jameson's, hardly a drop left, and there were crisp packets on the floor and two empty tumblers on the mantelpiece.

His feet were hard and quick on the stairs as he ran down to her voice. Coming into the living room he was a mess, unshaven, gaunt, eyes deep and dark, his hair unwashed for probably a week. He had the same Led Zeppelin T-shirt he had worn for days, even though it was too tight really and she could see his belly poking down out of the bottom.

"Kyle," he said, smiling, his eyes glazed. "Why you home so late?" The question was loose and distant like he was only half aware she had been gone. An echo of the dad he used to be.

He hugged her and she could smell the whisky and cigarettes.

"Where've you been all night? I was getting worried." His words slurring like melting ice running down a gutter, trickling.

"You didn't ring, Dad." She wanted to break free of his hug but instead she let him hold her.

He pulled away, frowning. "No, you're right, I didn't. I should have, I know I should have, Kyle, but I was busy."

He pushed past her, stumbled towards the table. There were papers scattered over it, his notebooks, the same as there was every night. His writing, a story maybe about the future, or just printouts from websites he'd found where someone else somewhere else in the world thought the same things he did. He rustled through them, papers falling to the rug.

"Look," he said, holding one piece out. She could see it was a printout but he had written on it, scribbled crazily all over it so half the page was covered in his words. "I was right, Kyle. I knew I was right but I didn't think we'd need to leave so soon. Turkey, I knew it would be something like Turkey. You see when somewhere is on the edge it's always ready to break. Just a tiny spark, that's all."

Her heart was racing, hammering at her chest as if it wanted to get free and not hear what she knew he was going to say. *Let me out, let me out before he breaks everything.*

"What are you saying, Dad?" she said, trying to keep her voice calm though she could feel tears welling in her eyes. He had been worse than this many times before. Ranting, crying, hitting the walls until his knuckles were red. So bad that she would lock herself in her bedroom, not because she was scared he would hurt her but because all his words did damage enough on their own. She hated him when he was like this. Hated seeing him so different to the dad who had been the only one there for her, read *Room on the Broom* to her and drew pictures of Torres over and over again for hours and never complained, tipped all the spices from the kitchen cupboards into a big bowl and made spicy pie just to entertain her. Madness, that's what it was; she knew it was that even though the doctor called it something else. She hated it more than she could ever hate anything. She wanted to get him and shake him or hug him, do anything to make it stop. But the truth was no shaking or hugging or medicine ever made him better. This was just him now. That old dad, the one who would daub and smear his face with the spicy pie mix and run around the kitchen whooping and pretending to be an American Indian, was gone.

He scratched at his hair, flecks of dandruff falling to the black of his T-shirt.

"I was right, I was absolutely right. We're not safe here so you see it's so simple, so obvious. We have to go away. Me and you, we're leaving here and we'll be safe then, more than safe. This world, here, everything around us and everything out there, it's all ending, Kyle. All of it."

She looked at the suitcases and knew one was packed full of her things, that he had gone into her room and filled it full of her things. She looked at him. He was pouring himself another whisky, his hand trembling. She thought of Spencer. When he said *Thursday* and she had known that she would meet him and they would walk, talk again even though she wasn't sure she would know what to talk about, that had felt like the beginning of something. Not love or anything that big, she wasn't as romantic as Hannah or as hopeful as Cerys. Just the start of a speck of life, a tiny microbe ready to grow and expand, live and be.

"Don't worry, I'll keep you safe, Kyle," her dad said. "I always promised you that, didn't I? I always said nothing bad would ever happen to you and it won't, not ever."

Maybe it was the cold, being out so long just stood in the cold and listening to people talk about something as cold as a life ending, her body too chilled deep at its core to let the warmth of the house energise her, wake her, but she was very tired all of a sudden. Her body felt slow and heavy, falling but not falling. She let her arms hang at her sides, her eyelids begged to close, her feet were like two slabs pulling her down into the floor. *No, I'll keep you safe, Dad.* She turned away and forced her leaden legs to climb the stairs. Halfway up there was a painting of Jesus. Her dad never went to church or made her go but he had promised her Nan that he would never take it down. It was a horrible painting and had always terrified Kyle but now as she looked at it she was only puzzled. It showed Jesus, staring out vacantly into nothing. He reminded her a little of the Mona Lisa, feminine, the thin wrist of his hand, his delicate fingers held up in blessing. It was his chest that had always frightened her. It wasn't horrific, torn open and gushing blood like a wild animal or a psychopath had gone at it. The thing that always scared her was that for some reason Jesus' heart was floating outside of his body, over his chest, and there was a flame on top of it like it was burning or being cooked right while he just stood there looking holy and these rays of light shone from the heart, light that didn't even come from the flames but from the heart itself. She frowned at the dust-covered painting, kept fighting back the tears that had been trying to come since he first spoke. Why would anyone do that, why would a person take their heart out and think it was a good thing and why would anyone want a painting of that? Sometimes she wondered how the world ever kept on going when people could imagine things like that.

When she was in her bed she pulled her duvet over her head and let everything become completely dark. She could hear him moving about downstairs so she closed her eyes tight, as if doing that would make the dark deeper. She thought of a Physics lesson she'd had last week, of dark matter and the parts of space that were completely empty of anything. How common that was, how much utter emptiness there was in the universe and how no one knew why there was so much of it. Her grandad knew all about physics but she doubted even he would be able to explain to her why the universe held so much darkness. She wanted a little bit of that for herself now, so she scrunched her eyes up tighter and tried to will some of it towards her, down through space, down through the atmosphere, down through the never- ending snow, down through her window and into her body.

But she knew the truth of things now like she had never known the truth of anything else. It was light flooding the dark but a light that was bad and hurt her eyes, burned into her. Filling the empty spaces with light when they never asked to be filled. Her dad was right, they needed to go away for a while at least to be safe. Not safe from bombs or war or hordes of extremists or the world ever ending. Just for him to get better. For him to be safe and happy. If they didn't go away now she knew he would only get worse and one day she wouldn't have him, like how she didn't have her Mum or Skan anymore. He would really be gone and she wouldn't even have a phone number that never answered or a cruel card.

I'll keep you safe, Dad. She said that over and over, whispering it to her deep dark until sleep brought quietness.

Chapter Four

Selny was the place where all the old magic escaped to when it was pushed out of Britain. An ever advancing shield-wall of the new, pushing and pushing its way across hills and moors, through the valleys and along the many rivers, until the blades and axes, the blood and steel, came to a cliff and with one final push all the magic that had once been constant across the land was gone forever. Caught by the tide, washed out and away, tossed and borne west until it found another place, an older place, a place where there was no one who wanted to push at the things they didn't understand or make something new that wasn't in the image of the old. A place where there was magic still. West of Britain and south of the Isle of Man, a small piece of what once was.

Or at least that was how her dad told the story

but then he had always been very good at telling her stories.

She knew now that all her father's stories about Selny were just that; just stories. Stories he made up to make her say, *Is that for real, Daddy?* And he would always hold her hand, give it one tight squeeze, and make his eyes go wide. *For real real,* he would say. It was the idea of there being an island not far away where there was magic, whatever magic was, that excited her so much on their first holiday to Selny. Even the name had seemed strange then, not magical maybe but a little song. *Selny.* When they were on the ferry that first time, her dad had shown her and Skan his old scrapbook, the front covered with stamps and Panini football stickers.

"We'd come here every summer to visit my Aunty Kate," he told them. "Me and your Uncle Owen would collect shells on Carow Beach, feathers too, catch some crabs maybe. Look at this one, that's a guillemot feather. Maybe we'll see some."

Guillemot. That too, strange, something other than the birds she saw every day and more of a song than pigeon and magpie, sparrow or seagull could ever be.

"We'll go to the stones," her dad had told them as they drove down from the ferry onto the docks of St Christopher, huddled granite fishing cottages hugging the quayside, old women wearing headscarves knitting outside the post office, fishermen mending nets with cigarettes trapped between their lips, the stink of fresh fish and the bells of the Little Chapel ringing for noon. "There're stones all over the island, must be about fifty different circles. No one knows why they're there, not really, they're not even sure who built them. I climbed on the Penny Stones once when I was your age, Skan, right to the top of the Sun Stone."

They were excited, both her and Skan restless to get out and see the island, watching the little town merge into low moors and scrub, then the road curved up to the cliffs and she could see black birds in the sky that weren't seagulls, she was sure of that, and down below were the waves, crashing against the rocks. Her dad had wound his window all the way down.

"Listen to that," he had shouted over the wind and they had listened. She heard it, the sea. The rise and crash, repeating, sounding so immeasurably strong.

But that was long ago.

She tossed her school bag to the back seat. She had made sure to pack that herself with some schoolwork, revision for the mock exams she hoped she would be back for, her Kindle and her iPad, her makeup, underwear and toiletries: things her dad wouldn't have thought to pack. Her mum's necklace was in there too, as well as the butterfly brooch Cerys had given her for her birthday and the money she had been saving. She wasn't sure why she had started saving the money, a few pounds here and there. Skan had done the same in the months before he left. He had shown her his stash in the bottom drawer of his wardrobe one Saturday morning.

"Never tell Dad," he had warned her. "Never let on."

By the time Skan left he'd managed to stash £500 from working the paper round and glass collecting in The Red Lion. She had counted what money she had this morning. £75. It was hardly enough to be running away with but she was sure she wouldn't do that. It was just in case, that was all. Just in case she really needed it.

"We ready?" said her dad.

He was different this morning. Calm and normal, almost like every other dad. He'd shaved and showered, the Led Zeppelin T-shirt left in the washing basket because probably he didn't mind the world ending and evaporating it or whatever he thought was going to happen. He was wearing the shirt he only ever wore to parents' evening and his old work blazer, his thinning hair neatly combed to one side. He looked well and she hadn't been able to say that for too long. That scared her more than anything else because she knew what it meant. It meant he was certain, so certain of everything that had filled up his head; that he had tricked himself into thinking he was fine, calm and normal.

She looked back at the house. She knew she would be back there, of course she knew. *This is just a holiday to make Dad better.* But as she looked up at the bay window of her bedroom, she saw the teddy bear Skan had bought her when she five and wondered if she should run up and get it. She looked at the teddy, trying to figure out if it meant anything to her, wondering if the world really did end would she miss it. *Yes.* Because it was Skan who had taught her to write her name on the label, backwards K and spidery E. *But the world won't end, not now, not ever.*

Her dad put his arm around her shoulder and she couldn't help but smell the aftershave he had drenched himself in.

"Wasn't a bad house, was it?" he said. He was smiling. He was about as happy as she had seen him in years. "Shame really, but there it is. Nothing stands forever."

She looked at the chipping green paint on the windowsill, the cream curtains drawn shut in the living room, the white tiles with number 54 painted on them. "What will happen to it?"

His arm stayed around her shoulder. She was tense, closed up. "It won't stand, not even bricks will stand." He sounded like a prophet. She hated that sound in his voice, that horrible certainty.

She pulled herself away and as she got into the car she took out her phone and snapped a picture of the house, zooming in to her window and the lonely teddy bear, its back to them. She uploaded it to her Instagram with a sad face. No one knew where she was going. She hadn't told Cerys or Hannah; she hadn't even told Spencer she wouldn't meet him after school. Her dad had rung in and simply told school she was ill.

"It won't matter that you won't be coming back," he had told her. "They can't fine me if the school's not there anymore."

He had laughed at that like it was a joke, and she hoped that maybe he was trying to make this less scary than he must have felt it was. He believed the world was ending, completely, utterly. Maybe he was trying to protect her from how massive that was but when she imagined the school being gone, just rubble or ash or something, she knew that couldn't be. The school wouldn't go, the village wouldn't go, the world wouldn't go. The only thing she was sure would go away was her dad's illness, finally and forever. That was what she had to do now, make him better, keep him safe. *I promise.*

They drove to the Aldi in town and stocked up. She had watched a film once about the world ending where people rioted over water and fought over tins of beans but there was no rioting in Aldi. They walked around the shop slowly filling the trolley but her dad wouldn't buy anything fresh, not even milk.

"UHT," she said, putting the tenth carton in the trolley. "It's disgusting. Won't we have a fridge?"

He laughed. "What good is a fridge when there's no power left?"

"Can we at least get some crisps and biscuits? They don't need a fridge." "As long as we get plenty of Jaffa Cakes."

At the till, the checkout girl scanned bottle after bottle of water. "Something you know I don't?" she joked.

"Plumbing disaster," her dad said.

The checkout girl shook her head and kept scanning. By the time they drove out of town towards the new bridge, the car was so full of shopping bags that she couldn't see out of the back window. She wondered for a moment if the police would stop them for that, like it was against the law to obscure a back window so much, and she wondered too whether if they did she would say something. *My dad has gone crazy and is taking me out of school to hide on an island until the world ends.* Maybe that would be best. At least he would get help then. But as she looked at him, his fingers tapping the wheel as the radio played a song he would never have hummed along with last week, she knew she would never do that. *I'm the only help he needs.*

"What about Skan?" she asked as they neared Runcorn. He didn't answer.

"Dad," she said after too much silence. "Did you ring him at least? Did you tell him? I was going to but I didn't know if you would want me to. Dad, did you?"

Again silence.

"Do you know," he said eventually, "at this exact moment there are four thousand NATO soldiers being deployed to Tallinn and at least double that in Russian soldiers lined up on the Estonian border. Just like that, someone decides to make a war happen and within hours it's happening, Kyle."

He shook his head and whistled through his teeth, reached out to turn the radio louder as it played *Uptown Funk.* "Do you know what, I actually quite like this."

It was late by the time they reached the bridge,

the traffic blocked up all the way back along the
expressway, every lane feeding in full of stuck cars
as the sun set a brilliant red in the clear winter sky.
There was no snow today and not a single cloud. The
sky was like a lake of ice, coldest blue, and the world
looked like it went on and on, unending. The huge
chimneys of the power plant let out plumes of smoke,
tinged with fire by the sun so it seemed like four squat
dragons, mouths gaping, breathed their fire into the
sky. She pulled her coat close about herself and tried
not to feel so small, but as their car crawled closer to
the bridge and she saw that the river too was alive
with oranges and reds, she couldn't stop looking at
the sun, hanging there, gradually fading and colouring
the world as it left the day. From the east there were
purples and blurred blues reaching out, bringing
evening, and the vapour trails of planes crisscrossed
the sky like scratches on a perfect face. She closed her
eyes and tried to imagine that their car was all there
was in the world but it was no good; no matter how
much she tried to make herself feel small and believe
that, she could still feel the vastness of the world, the
wide open sky, the jet streams that told the stories of
other lives being lived, movement and motion, hear
the radio, a woman's voice, her dad's fingers tapping.
She opened her eyes and gave in. By the time they
drove into Liverpool and along Hope Street, parking

beside the cathedral just opposite her grandparents' house, it was evening and dark.

She hadn't seen her grandparents for nearly a year but the house was the same as always. A grand townhouse, high steps leading to a black door, freshly coated judging from the sheen of gloss, the lion knocker in its centre, the lion fiercely biting down on an iron ring. There was a basement they sublet to students from the university, fresh flowers in the low windows, and the attic was where she and Skan would always sleep, high up with the sash window overlooking the graveyard in the hollow beside the cathedral. The curtains, thick and red, were all drawn to keep out the night, but as her dad opened the wrought iron gate it set a little bell to ring and a light came on in the hall. The door was opened by the time they were at the steps and there were her grandparents, her mother's parents, as old as they ever looked. Her gran was smiling, eyes moist so Kyle wondered if she had been crying or if that was just what happened to your eyes when you got old.

"My, you're a sight for sore eyes," said her gran, taking Kyle's hand. Her hand felt so fragile, small, and Kyle tried to remember if it had always felt like that. Yes, her mum's hands had been like that too. Fragile, the skin rice paper-thin, the light blue of veins almost shining out. Now her gran's hand was scattered with liver spots and as she hugged Kyle, there was the old scent of Estée Lauder perfume. Kyle pushed her head close to her cardigan.

"We've missed you so very much," said her gran.

"I've missed you too." It wasn't true, not really. There were some days when she knew she should call them, or worse than that when they would ring her phone and she would ignore it. She was never sure why. It wasn't like she blamed them for her mum going; that happened long ago and they had been forever in her and Skan's lives after that. It was only really since Skan had left that Kyle had stopped visiting them, stopped knowing with the certainty she had in childhood that she should love them. There had been a day, a week after Skan had phoned to say he had found a place in Brixton, when her grandad came to the house and for an hour there was shouting. She had heard something break and bad words, words she never thought her grandad could say. Now he stood with his arms out and she let him hug her.

"Where've you been, lass?" he said, his voice still tinged and layered with the soft lyrical tones of the Western Isles. He moved back and looked at her, his brow furrowed, his puffy lips dry and chapped. "You're well, aren't you?" And then he looked past her to her dad and his frown turned to a scowl.

She knew what he meant. *Do you really want to go with him?*

"I'm fine, Grandad."

"Aye, well maybe we can all have a wee chat and catch up. We've supper in the oven if you're hungry."

Her gran's hand was on hers again, china fingers curling about it. "You're staying the night, aren't you?"

"The ferry is first thing in the morning, Moira," said her dad. He was calm, almost robotic. Like there was nothing wrong with him at all, like in his mind somewhere there wasn't this tumour of a thought that everything was about to end. "I thought you'd like to see Kyle before we left."

Her grandad's scowl deepened. "Aye, you did. Well come on in inside, it's a dire night."

The hall was long, chequered black and white tiles running its length, and there were some of her gran's paintings on the walls as well as a framed letter written to her grandad from Stephen Hawking and another picture of her grandad with a tall, bald man who Kyle guessed was another famous physicist. There was a picture of her mum and uncles when they were little beside that. It had always been in that same spot, like Jesus and his burning heart, but she wouldn't look at it.

They ate pastitsio and her grandparents asked her about school.

"Science, is it?" said her grandad, happy. "I always hoped your mother had my scientific leanings; maybe they skipped a generation."

Her gran touched her hand again. She had been doing it all through dinner, reaching out to her as if she was checking she was real, solid and actually there. Or maybe it was to hold on to her, thought Kyle. Maybe the next time she touched her hand she would hold it hard and refuse to let go, anchor her to them.

She patted Kyle's hand tenderly. "There's more to the world than atoms and quarks, Alistair."

Her grandad pushed his fork into his salad and lifted up a slither of balsamic-drenched radish. "Aye there is, but nothing quite as grand as knowing why every little thing came to be."

"What about the bigger things?" put in her dad. "You don't need a microscope to see what the world is made up of."

Her grandad sighed and laid his fork calmly on his plate. "I prefer to look a little deeper than what's right in front of me to find my answers."

Her dad had hardly eaten. "You can't just ignore what's going on around you, Alistair. That's the problem with this world, too many people closing their eyes."

Her grandad picked up his water and sipped it. He

only ever drank water, not even tea or coffee, just water. "Jon, I can only hope that one day, for Kyle's sake if not your own, you start to see that it does no good at all to imagine all the monsters of the world coming to your doorstep. If that happens, it happens. In the meantime, all we can do is look closer at our own lives and keep hold of what good we have. You have so much good, you always have."

No one spoke. She could hear the clock on the mantelpiece ticking and a cat crying in the alleyway behind the house.

Her grandad looked at her. "Are you sure you want to go, Kyle? You can stay with us if you want, focus on your schoolwork. Surely, you've too much on to miss a day, let alone a week."

Kyle looked to her dad. Even in his best shirt, even without the stubble and stained T-shirt, she could see the truth of him in his eyes. They were so tired, so sad. He couldn't hide that from her no matter how hard he tried to hide it from her grandparents, it was the him that had been around for too many years now to suddenly just vanish.

"It was my idea," she said quickly, looking from her gran to grandad. "I asked Dad could we go, you know, back to Selny because of all the holidays we used to have. We haven't been anywhere for ages and I've got all the work I need with me. I haven't had a day

64

off since Year Seven; it's hardly going to make me fail my GCSEs missing a week at the end of term is it? Besides, the doctor says Dad needs a break and I want us to have a nice Christmas, I want him to be better. All we're doing is going away for a week, there's no harm in that."

Her grandad went to say something but her gran cut him off. "Listen to the girl, Alistair. She knows her own mind. I think she's right, maybe the two of us should follow her example and have ourselves a wee holiday."

Nothing more was said about Kyle staying. They ate a lemon tart her gran had made, the pastry as delicate as her hands, and the cream flavoured with whisky. The tart seemed to calm them all down and by the time their plates were empty it was like she was sat around a table with a normal family who did this all the time. No frowns, no scowls, no stubbornness. Just tea and words. It felt strange, out of place and false, and soon her feet began to jitter and shift beneath the table, desperate for a cigarette. She looked at her dad, smiling and talking about football, about Hibernian getting knocked out of the cup, as if everything was really normal, as if they had all only seen each other just yesterday, and her grandparents smiling politely back because they were nice people, good people, and this was how good people behaved.

Even though there was more than a gap of years between them all. There was a hole, something missing, and not one of them mentioned it, not one of them mentioned her mother's name.

"I might go for a walk," she said. She wanted to smoke but that was only to get away and leave the falseness of them. It wasn't really the need to smoke that made her leg shake. It was that they had no right to pretend there wasn't a chunk of all of them missing.

"Ah, but do you not think it's late, Kyle?" said her gran. "Wouldn't you prefer me to show you your room? I bought you some new bedding, just in case. We couldn't have you sleeping in a *Power Rangers* bed at your age could we?"

"She'll be fine," said her dad. "Just don't be too long, Kyle. I need to talk to your grandparents in private anyway."

She wondered if they were going to talk about her mum but then she realised the idea was ridiculous. Why all of a sudden talk about something you had refused to even acknowledge for over a decade? She could guess what her dad wanted to talk about. Money. Her grandparents had lots of it and they had so little. The end of the world was probably an expensive thing to run away from.

Her gran touched her hand one last time and

looked at her so deep in her eyes that she wanted to turn away. "Don't go too far," she said and she kissed Kyle softly on her forehead.

Kyle lit a cigarette as soon as the little bell on the gate had rung behind her. The pavement was slippery with ice so she walked slowly along Hope Street, looking up at the townhouses and wondering what types of people lived there. One house had shutters instead of curtains and another had a huge terracotta Buddha in the drive. Another had eight different buzzers on the intercom and every window had different curtains. The house at the end was shabby, an old Saab rusting out front. At the end of the street she saw a group of tourists standing around a woman who was dressed all in black with a tall hat and white, ghostly face, her hands waving dramatically as she ushered them along the street towards the Catholic cathedral. She crossed to the Anglican and leaning on the railings she looked up at it. It was so high, so out of place. Liverpool never seemed like an old city to her, everything was too new, even in the streets around her grandparents' house. But the cathedral was like some fantastical castle, towering and gothic, imposingly dark against the black sky. She blew out smoke between the railings. There were no birds flying above the high central tower but she imagined there should be crows circling it, a whole murder of them just whirling and whirling about the tower, ever circling. It didn't look a good place, not like a church should look. It looked a bad and secret place where anything might be happening. She looked down into the graveyard, little tombs dotted about, forgotten, uncherished, grey obelisks and squat plinths, graves leaning into each other with names too weathered to know.

This wasn't Liverpool, she told herself, this was another place, a shadow world, a Shadow Liverpool. She looked up at the cathedral. There were crows, hundreds of them circling the tower. They were a demon's servants and if she were foolish enough to drop her cigarette and let herself be lured down into the graveyard there would be monsters waiting and the dead would want her to join them. She turned around and leaned back against the railings, looked at the posh town houses and imagined that they were all ruins, shells of what they had once been, like the old church down the hill; hollows, broken and useless. The whole city was that: a ruined place of too much evil, and she was alone, vulnerable. At any moment there might be howling and when the wolves came out of the alleys and ginnels she would have no one to save her but herself.

She dropped her cigarette and kicked it into the street. She took out her phone and took a photograph of the shabby house and uploaded it to her Instagram, tagging it with "My Hero", wondering if Spencer would get that.

Her grandparents' front door was unlocked so she let herself in. She could hear the three of them talking, her dad's voice loudest but still calm. She climbed the stairs all the way to the attic and opened the door to her bedroom. All of her and Skan's old toys were gone, the board games and even the Xbox. There was a new brown rug and her bedding was Kath Kidston. She undressed to her underwear and got into the warm bed. There was a small table beside it, different to the one that used to be there, and as she reached to turn the bedside lamp off she noticed there was a book with a folded piece of paper on top.

Kyle, I thought this might remind you of your mum and us. Love always, Granny xxx

It was an old edition. The corners were frayed and a little dog-eared. The cover showed a Roman soldier wearing some kind of animal as a cloak and holding a staff with a gold eagle at its top and a small sword in his other hand. *The Eagle of the Ninth.*

"Skan maybe," she said quietly. It was Skan who had always read the book to her, not her mum. She didn't have that memory like her gran thought she did, no memory of songs to lull her to sleep even. Her mum had left and with her had gone anything to fasten those memories too, so that as the years passed, whatever memory she had left of her became a ghost, fainter and fainter, until Kyle was unsure of what was a memory and what was a dream, made up to fill the gaps.

She opened the first page and there at its top was perfectly neat and scrolling writing in green pen. *Paisley Smith, Liverpool, July 15th 1984.* She switched off the light and turned on to her side, holding the book close to her body.

Chapter Five

She watched the city slowly disappear into the morning mist as the SeaCat moved smoothly out into Liverpool Bay, towards the bitter winds that were sweeping south across the Irish Sea.

When they were in the hold, her dad had turned Radio 4 up for the news. A clipped voice spoke.

"…NATO stated today that the rising tensions between Russia and the West were a matter for diplomacy not idle threats, as the Russian President, Vladimir Putin, declared the shooting down of a Russian Su-34 fighter bomber on the Turkey/Syria border ten kilometres from the Turkish city of Gaziantep to be 'an act of aggression and a reckless movement towards avoidable escalations in violence'. The pilot of the Russian jet has been named as 34-year-old Ilya Krivulkin though it has not yet been declared if the rumours that he was killed after the jet was shot down are true. Meanwhile, the UK Ambassador to Lithuania has today asked…"

Kyle had taken out her phone and tried her best to ignore the woman's words but they wouldn't completely leave her. *War, the UN, the situation in Estonia, support of President Assad, the American President stated, no room for negotiation, unacceptable, final warning.*

She had looked at Spencer's Instagram, tried to zoom in to the idea of him, tried to imagine what it would have been like to walk with him, talk more to him, but the radio kept pulling her away. Back into the world. She rummaged in her coat pocket for headphones and plugging them into the phone she searched Spotify for the band he said he liked. As the music played she closed her eyes and rested her head back, and when the song was over she played it again. She could see him, cocooned within himself, moving almost against the world on his way to school. Through the village, the woods, along the canal, slow, alone.

Her dad had tapped her arm, pulling her away from her own cocoon of images.

"Why don't you go up to the restaurant, see the view?" he said.

She took off her headphones so the song became

muffled, distant like Spencer, fainter still as the headphones dangled in her lap. "What about you?"

"I might just sleep for a bit."

The deep shadows beneath his eyes were darker today. When she had woken early, saw on her phone that it was only four o'clock, she had heard him in the room below her, a low whisper as if he was talking to someone, though she could make out no words, just a hum of whispers. He was hasty to go all morning, trying his best to hide his fears, to not show her grandparents that they were running.

She sat in the empty restaurant watching England disappear. Her coffee was cold, the croissant only once bitten. It was cold too in the restaurant even though there were radiators. The tables were dingy, their bright laminate tops peeling to reveal the ugly grey beneath, and when her knee had touched the underside of the table she had felt something sticky there and jerked her leg away. Her phone was on the table, the phone number ready to be rung. She tapped the screen to wake it, saw the pale blue square with the small white writing. Finally, she had made herself save the number. *Mum.* Her finger hovered over the little green phone but for too long; the screensaver kicked in and the phone went black. *There's no difference.* For all the times she had tried ringing that number, the phone might as well have stayed black, dead. Sometimes she wondered if it was really was her mum's number, but then it would ring every time she rang it so, she rationalised, it must have been somebody's number. She would tell herself, torture herself, that a phone doesn't stay on forever without somebody charging it. That made her sadder than anything. That somewhere, her mum was seeing this same number ring and never once thought to answer.

"Block me then," she said, pushing her phone far across the table so it nearly fell off the edge, slowing to a stop.

"Sometimes all we need is an answer," said a voice and she jumped, knocking her coffee so the cold liquid leapt from the cup.

She looked up. There was a dark-skinned man in his forties, standing beside her table. He was wearing a tweed jacket and maroon jumper with a shirt and chintzy bow tie. He had greenish cords on. His hair was grey at the temples and he was smiling, showing teeth that were perfectly white except for one of his front teeth which had been broken, cracked in half so a jagged remnant remained.

"Forgive me," he said, his accent strange. She couldn't place it, he looked Middle Eastern but then he might have been North African. She knew there were lots of immigrants; some of the boys in her year never stopped going on about them like they were scared that all these dark people would come and just by being there somehow make their skin darker, change them and the country. She remembered, through the echo of her father's anger at the leavers, the referendum and the queues of people outside the church hall. Her dad was sure all of them were voting to leave, voting to build a wall up around the whole country so no one else could get in, no matter how much those people needed somewhere to go. Rose, her grandparents had been Polish but she couldn't speak Polish. She was just another girl and now she was dead and everyone was sad; no one cared that her surname was Nowak.

The stranger was holding a cup of coffee. "I never sit alone when I drink coffee; this life is too short for drinking coffee alone."

Without asking he sat himself down at the table. His coffee was oil black, steam rising from it. It looked warmer than the room ever could be. He lifted the cup and sipped, looking at her as he sipped.

"You do not mind do you?" he asked.

She reached across the table for her phone. "No, I'm going anyway." "But your coffee?" he said.

She put her phone away. "It's gone cold. I don't really like coffee."

The strange man laughed. "How often have I heard

that in England? You people are always going out for coffee but I don't think any of you truly appreciate coffee. Now tea, that is your great love."

She didn't stand. Her first thought had been to get away as quickly as possible but as he sipped his coffee again she didn't feel any need to run. He wore a bow tie, yes, but all he seemed to want to do was sit and drink his coffee, not try to grope her legs like someone had groped Charlotte Massey's legs last Halloween on the train to Knutsford.

"Do you go to Selny?" he asked, making the island sound exotic, sounding the s and making the last syllable stretch.

She nodded. She lifted her coffee and sipped it. It was freezing and tasted like the cheap ground stuff her dad would always buy from Tesco. The stranger laughed.

"Maybe I am wrong. Maybe some of you do appreciate good coffee or at least, thank god, you recognise bad coffee."

He laughed again and put down his cup, slowly, deliberately. He was sitting very stiffly, almost in opposition to his cheeriness, and his movements were precise, slightly robotic, as if each stretch of the arm, each arching of an eyebrow or curl of fingers about the coffee cup was planned and followed through with that same deliberateness.

"Who do you go to Selny with?" he asked.

She took another sip of her coffee but it didn't taste any better. "My dad. We're going on holiday but we come here a lot."

He nodded. "A holiday is a good thing. I am going to Selny for my first time." He held up a finger and she noticed the top was missing. Like it had been sliced off just below the nail. "I said to myself only a week ago, I said Barzelay, you must have a holiday but I have very little money so there will be no half-the-world-away holiday for me, just a small trip. But I have heard great things about Selny."

Kyle couldn't think of too many great things about Selny. They had gone there for so many summers that all the things she thought were great that first time became boring. The last time they went all she did was sit in her room playing *Minecraft* on her laptop while her dad drank whisky in the garden. The lighthouse, the cliffs, the pretty granite cottages, the circles of stone, the old carvings that her dad had told her were runes. By that last trip there was hardly a bit of magic left in any of it.

"It's nice," she said. "It's old."

He laughed again. It was a quiet sort of laugh, subtle, not harsh like Spencer's or worrying like her dad's. It was a laugh that had been laughed many times. She felt oddly comfortable with the man even though she had always hated it when strangers tried to talk to her.

"Yes, old," he said. "But all the world is old. No, I think Selny deserves a better description than this. I have read that Selny is an echo of a lost world. I like the idea of this. There should be more places where what once was still remains. Do you not think?"

"I don't think there's anywhere really like that," she said. She knew she should get up and go back to the car just in case he was one of those types of men that Cerys was always saying were everywhere. The ones Cerys somehow always managed to sit next to on the bus who smiled at her and made sure they hardly moved out of the way at all when she had to get past. But she stayed. The SeaCat was powering on deeper into the Irish Sea; fat and full grey- black clouds were hanging low over the water. She had nowhere to be but here.

"Ah, a pessimist," he laughed. "Barzelay was once like you but very soon I understood that the world is too surprising to always live in fear of what might be. We must let go of all that nonsense and embrace the wonder of things. Take the rabbits for example, you have heard of the rabbits of Selny of course?"

She shook her head and he laughed again.

"What? You have not heard of the rabbits? My God but it is a wonderful tale. Did you know that

Selny once did not have any rabbits, not a single one? This was as late as the 19th century, not such a very long time ago at all, and do you know why that is so peculiar?"

She shook her head again. "Because rabbits breed so quickly?"

He smiled. He had a constant look of wonder and joy in his eyes. "Not at all. It is so peculiar because of one incredible fact. May I?"

He pointed to her coffee and when she said nothing he reached out and, lifting it, carefully tipped a little pool of it onto the table. He placed the cup back gently onto its saucer and then with his tip-shorn finger he began to draw on the table with the milky coffee, dragging the liquid one way then another, and up once and down, then up and down again, until he had drawn out what looked to Kyle like a rabbit's head with the ears cast back, one smaller than the other.

"Do you see?" he said, taking an unblemished handkerchief from the inside pocket of his blazer and cleaning the coffee from his finger.

"It's a rabbit's head," she said.

"Exactly!" he shouted and he pointed excitedly to the coffee drawing. "This is Selny. An island born from the sea and shaped by God or time to resemble a rabbit's head. Maybe, even before there were rabbits on this world, fate had it that a whole island was created in the image of rabbits. Don't you think that remarkable? But what is more remarkable than that is that despite the rapid spread, the incredibly proficient adeptness at breeding of rabbits throughout the world, despite the Romans bringing them to Britain and the little creatures spreading like wildfire everywhere they laid their paws, not one rabbit came to Selny. Not on a boat or as a pet or by some strange chance, in all of history. What is this called? I know the word, I know it. Ah, yes, it is a paradox. Would you not say so?"

Paradox. She knew what that meant from Miss Cunningham's SPAG challenges in Year Eight. *Two opposite facts clashing, like how someone could love someone so much they had to leave.* That's what Skan used to say. Mum left us because she loved us too much.

"But then how did the rabbits reach Selny?" said Barzelay, his eyes wide, excited by his own story now. "In the city where I was born we had monks, Coptics, and there was one particular monk who liked to keep rabbits as pets. Maybe monks are very fond of rabbits. Or maybe there is some Christian symbolism in rabbits that Barzelay does not understand, but in 1865 a Benedictine monk named Brother Cassian saw it as his duty to God to populate the isle of Selny with rabbits for, and this is the most intriguing part to my own little mind, he believed that God would not have created an island to so closely resemble a rabbit's head only to leave it so bereft of rabbits. He saw it as God's mission for him and so he brought a hundred rabbits to the isle, and within ten years there were a thousand and within a hundred they had multiplied beyond count because there are only foxes on Selny and very few birds of prey, not a single snake. One rabbit begot another and another and another until the whole island was full of begotten rabbits."

Barzelay gave a loud laugh and slapped his hand down to his corduroy trousers.

But Kyle only frowned. "Why would he do that? There was no need for him to do that, it wouldn't have made any difference if there were no rabbits."

Barzelay nodded and drank the last of his coffee. When he was finished he dabbed his lips with the handkerchief and sighed. "It is a good story but I see what you are saying. Humans, we are forever doing unfathomable things, things which make others question why or wonder for what purpose these things are done. Believe me when I say I have spent these last years wondering that same thing about many events. Have you heard of sanctuary?"

"When you ask a church to keep you safe?"

"Exactly so. I am coming to Selny for a kind of sanctuary from all such questions and that is, I think, why I am liking this story so much and I think to myself, I think Barzelay go to this place and find what other stories of this kind you can dig up. It is a ridiculous story but perhaps I am in need of ridiculous things that make me smile."

Barzelay pointed to the large viewing window. The clouds were heavier, closer. "The BBC believed the weather would be calm on Selny today but it appears we will be having much rain. One can never trust a weatherman. In truth, I was hoping it would be better weather here. My brother would always say that the weather got better the further west you went but this is not true. The weather can be bad in whatever direction you travel."

He stared out of the window in silence for a moment. "Did you ever pray at the stones?"

She shook her head. "I don't think so. My dad said people used to pray at them, like Vikings and stuff, but I've never seen anyone praying there."

Barzelay took a long, deep breath. "I was considering that when I reached these stones I would pray but I was not sure what to pray for. Maybe I will pray for better weather. That or pray that I am not run down by these wild horses I have read about. I hear there are many accidents with wild horses on Selny and I am afraid to say, I have never liked horses"

He laughed and stood, smoothing down his blazer and dabbing at his lips again with the handkerchief. He wasn't tall, he was slight and thin. She saw now that his left hand was held close to his side and she wondered if in the whole time he was sat at the table he had lifted it once. If he had she hadn't noticed. The arm looked heavy, like it was always there in that position, clinging to his side.

"I must leave you alone now," he said, smiling, his eyes grey and sad like her dad's. That was something she could see easily in a person from all the years of seeing it in her dad's own eyes. That sadness that doesn't shift, stays there, locked in the eyes no matter how much a person smiles. *I wonder if anyone sees that in my eyes.*

"I would ask you your name but sometimes it is good to be, how do you say, ships that pass in the night. Yes, we will be two ships upon a ship and I will say goodbye to you and wish you well."

He bowed his head a little and turned, his left arm still flat to his side. When he had left the restaurant, she looked at the coffee rabbit. He was right, there were so many rabbits on Selny. Once, she and Skan had come out into the garden of the cottage they were staying at and all the way down to the river there were rabbits. A garden of rabbits, Skan had called it. Even when she had shouted out *rabbits*, they hadn't run away like the rabbits did at home. They just stayed there, eating grass, secure in their numbers.

Skan ran back inside and returned with some pieces of carrot. He tossed one towards the nearest rabbit but it ignored the carrot and went on eating grass.

"Skan, why don't we ring Mummy and tell her about the rabbits? Maybe she'll come on holiday too, but we'd have to tell Daddy to go away for a bit."

Skan had thrown another piece, a little further, a little harder, so it bounced on the grass and made a small brown rabbit jump. "No, we don't need her anymore. It's okay, just you and me feeding them."

She reached out and carefully put her finger on the coffee stain rabbit. Slowly at first, she began to trace circles through the coffee and then faster until there was no rabbit, just circles within circles, overlapping and crossing and distorting.

Chapter Six

St Christopher was a harbour town, built for the
fishermen whose boats would sail out each dawn
through the Quiver Strait and past the little sister isle
of Darry and the rocky Arrowheads, north towards
Scotland to fish for haddock, cod and langoustines.
The walled harbour had one entry point, the Water
Gate, which had been widened after the war to
let ferries through. The town itself wasn't as old as
Brunden, the capital, which stood in the clawed grasp
of Brunden Bay, fifteen miles north east along the
coast. There were three thousand people in Brunden
and half that in St Christopher, but St Christopher
was where the tourists came because of the old granite
fishing cottages that lined the harbour front, and the
Mezzids, the narrow alleyways which burrowed back
into the town itself and were home to bistros and

restaurants, too many fishmongers and far too many candle shops, a deli or two and plenty of cafes. There were enough pubs in St Christopher alone to get everyone on the island well drunk twice over. On the harbour side there were six: The Salutation, The Irish Fleet, The Blue Ship, The Checky Cat, Ma Tadgett's and The Starry Hammer. Behind the harbour, the town rose up to the Holy Hills and much of the town proper was scattered about the nearest hill – Gad's Table – a plateau-topped hill whose south face was lined with fine townhouses that reminded Kyle of her grandparents' house. On the top of the hill there was the ruin of an ancient church, just a broken wall here and there and a half-collapsed spire. There was a funicular to take tourists to the top where they could be wind battered and try and fail to see Ireland on a good day.

Kyle sat on a bench outside the post office while her dad was inside buying cigarettes. She had almost asked him to get her twenty Marlboro. He couldn't mind her smoking if the world was ending, surely? Was there really any better time to smoke than right at the very end of everything? She doubted if there was but didn't risk asking him.

The weather had not yet broken, the sky was still fat with cloud and the town quiet, emptied of tourists for the winter. No one came to Selny in winter. No one was stupid enough to waste money coming. She read the plaque that was screwed to the bench. *For Jack Casker – he knew how to sit and wait.* That was a strange thing to be remembered for, doing nothing. She looked out to the harbour where there were a few boats tied up that looked like they hadn't been out for years and one old fisherman balling up nets and tossing them into the back of a dented van. There wasn't much to see. Poor Jack Casker. She hoped he had plenty to think about because St Christopher didn't offer much to entertain on its own. She sighed. She had doubted whether she had made the right choice to come ever since the ferry had passed Darry. It was a sudden and stark realisation that her dad might not get better, that she might be stuck here with him for weeks or months and that, deep down, she knew she would never leave him, not now, even if they were stuck here for ages, even if she had nothing to do, not even school to go to. No Cerys. No Hannah. No Spencer. She had messaged him on the ferry, told him she would be back next week. Asked him could they still meet, but the message hadn't delivered and the Wi-Fi signal on her phone had cut out altogether once they drove down the ferry ramp into St Christopher.

I'm not Jack Casker, she told herself, and stood up. There was a reason she was here and that reason was to help her dad. *I don't matter, not for a while at least, not until he's better.* She glanced into the post office and saw him talking to the owner. He looked happy. He was leaning against the counter and smiling as he talked. So normal. She couldn't hear his words but the owner wasn't looking at him like people usually looked at him, so she doubted he was talking about the end of the world. Probably football, probably some story about his holidays here.

She walked down the street a little way. There were puddles dotted about the cobbles from the melted snow and on some of the houses thin layers of snow still clung to the roof tiles, slowly and stubbornly melting. There was a bus stop and a tall boy was standing beneath its shelter. As she walked closer he started looking at her, not even subtly. Staring at her so she felt suddenly self-conscious that she wasn't wearing tights.

"Alright there," he said, still looking right at her, then down to her legs. He was about her age, maybe older. Tall but strong, broad, he had white-blonde hair and eyebrows that were hardly there. He was rough looking, stony. He was wearing a Barbour jacket that was a little too small for him and hoisted on his strong shoulders was a khaki backpack with a sleeping bag rolled and tied with frayed rope to its top. Against the bus stop rested an air rifle.

Even though he was looking at her so hard, hungrily, she stopped at the bus stop. "You just come in then? From ferry?"

He was looking at her face. That was worse, worse than him staring at her legs. He was looking right in her eyes, then at her lips. She felt like he was figuring her out, deciding something about her. She wasn't used to boys looking at her like that, even Spencer hadn't. Part of her wanted to turn around, walk away as quickly as possible but another part of her wanted to do nothing but stay there for a minute or two at least and let him look at her.

"Yeah," she said.

He nodded. "Where you come in from?"

Now she was closer to him she realised he was older, maybe eighteen. He had rough blonde stubble and there was a little scar on his cheek like a cross.

"We're from Cheshire," she said.

"Never been. Went to Liverpool once when I were five."

She didn't know what to say. Cerys would know. *Flirt*, she would have screamed at her if she was there, *for God's sake flirt with someone*. Why not, why shouldn't she? But he was still looking at her and she knew why; she knew what it was that made him look and what he probably wanted, even if he never said it, even if he just kept looking.

"You look like that one off *Harry Potter*, you know the one? The clever one."

No one had ever told her she looked like anyone. She smiled. That was right, Cerys always said you had to smile. "Hermione?"

He nodded again. "I reckon. Bit prettier, I'd say."

She pushed her hands into her pockets and felt her cheeks warming. The air rifle was close to her, just the butt showing, the rest wrapped tightly in a waterproof covering. "What's that for?"

He twitched one shoulder so his backpack jerked. "Rabbits. I shoot them, mostly"

His hand went into his coat pocket and he brought out a small flashlight that was attached to his keys. He flicked it on and the light that darted out of it was much brighter than she expected. "Army use these. SAS use them I reckon. I shine it at the rabbits and they freeze, freeze so they can't move 'coz they're scared of the light or something, then I can shoot them." He moved his shoulder again, indicating the back pack. "Got ten here."

She looked at the backpack, full, and saw the outlines of shapes crammed together like they were pushing against the material.

"You really do that?" she said.

He shrugged. "Got to eat. Too many rabbits

anyway, doing the council a favour. My mam makes proper good rabbit stew. I like rabbit stew."

His voice was slow, like he struggled over the words he wanted to say. He glanced down to her legs again.

"Don't suppose you shoot rabbits much in Cheshire."

She smiled just like Cerys would have wanted her to but it was a weak smile. All she could think about were the poor rabbits, all squashed together and dead. And this boy, looking at her without caring that she knew he was looking at her, like he had every right to look at her because she was there.

"I should go," she said and turned, trying not to think about him watching her as she went, pulling her coat down so it covered more of her back.

"Isaac," he called after her, but she didn't turn, just quickened her pace. She could see her dad coming out of the post office. "My name's Isaac Marcaret."

When she got to the car, her dad was looking past her to the bus stop. "What's he looking at? You weren't talking to him where you?"

She opened the car door quickly and got in. "No, I wasn't. He's just some boy that's all."

Her dad got in and started the engine up. "They're a weird lot over here, love. Just be careful who you

talk to, especially the boys; they probably haven't seen
someone as pretty as you that they weren't related to
in all their lives."

He laughed and turned the radio on. They had
to drive up the road towards the cliffs, west of St
Christopher, and that meant passing the bus stop. She
didn't mean to look at him, but as she looked down,
pretending to do something on her phone, she turned
a little to see him looking back. He nodded his head
and without knowing why she shook hers, smiling a
small smile, and then he was gone and within minutes
St Christopher was behind them. The road climbed
up into the moors with the Holy Hills beyond them.
Now the heavens finally opened and rain hammered
the windscreen so her dad had to drive slower, the car
struggling up the steep incline. He didn't wind the
window down when they neared the cliffs, too focused
on driving through the deluge, concentrating on the
road and the rain. Even the lighthouse was obscured
by the rain and by the time they drove the length of
the Cod Road towards Fishley where their cottage
was, there was something biblical about the rain.
*Maybe this is it, maybe this is how Dad knows the world
ends.* She doubted it. She knew her dad was more
scared of bombs and war than he was of God. No, a
flood would take the whole world away. Even Selny
would be drowned, that's what happened in the Bible.

The whole world drowned so you needed a boat just to survive.

The cottage was on the outskirts of the village. There was a grand house where her dad picked up the keys from a nervous-looking old woman, getting soaked as he ran from the car to the house and back again.

"The King of Jamaica is angry today," he shouted, grinning with his face dripping wet, as he got back in. That was what he would say to her when she was little whenever the weather was bad, really windy or rainy, when they were walking together and the wind would come from nowhere or the sky would burst open with rain. *The King of Jamaica is coming to get us, Kyle.* Back then she would scream and they would run through the rain together, holding hands, like the King of Jamaica was at their heels, trying to grab them and take them away.

"It's just rain, Dad," she said. She was looking at her phone. The Wi-Fi was working and the message to Spencer had delivered but he hadn't replied. She looked on Instagram and saw a link he had posted to a music video ten minutes earlier. She started typing another message, paused halfway through, and deleted it.

They drove down a long drive past a little lake towards the cottage. The cliffs were nearby and there were gulls over them, not guillemots, just gulls. When they finally reached the cottage it was small, more of a summer house really. The outside was covered in creepers stripped of their leaves. The front door was a fading green and the net curtains looked an unwashed and unhealthy yellow.

"Listen to me, Kyle," her dad said once they were parked outside the cottage. He reached for her hand and squeezed it. "I want you to know that I'm going to look after you. I know you've thought in the past that I wasn't well and you were right, everyone was right about that. But I want you to know that whatever happens I'll keep you safe because you're my little girl and you're all I have in this world. I promise."

He squeezed her hand again. She couldn't look at him, she only kept looking down at her phone. She wondered if he would hug her. It had been ages since they had hugged, so long that she couldn't even remember the last time he had held her.

"I know," she mumbled. "You don't have to tell me."

He didn't let go of her hand. "I just wanted to say it, that's all. I just wanted you to know that all this, coming here, taking you away from your home and your friends, I'm doing it for you and you alone. You know that don't you? I'm doing it to keep you safe."

She nodded, not looking up. "I know that."

He gave her hand one last squeeze. "Good, I'm glad you do. We'll be safe, we'll be happy. Everything will be okay, I promise."

She nodded again. *I promise, I promise.* He was right, everything would be okay, she would make sure of that, and when they went back home everything would only get better and maybe Skan would see that. Maybe, by some miracle, her mum would see that, somehow. *I promise, I promise.*

The rain was still going strong, relentless. "One, two, three and we run for it," he said. "I'll get everything in later."

He counted. One. Two. Three. Then they were out, running as fast as they could to the front door. The rain soaked them, finding a way through her coat and as he fumbled over the key she noticed there was a ceramic house sign beside the faded green door. It didn't have a number, just the house's name. She read it and then read it again. Painted beside the words was a rose, a red rose.

Rose Cottage, she mouthed. It didn't seem right or possible, even though she knew it was just a coincidence, just chance. *Rose Cottage.* It was just a name that lots of houses had, she knew that. No, it meant nothing else, nothing.

"Come on," she pleaded, anxious to get away from

the painted rose, the black letters. "I'm trying. I'm trying."

At last he opened the door and she pushed past him into the dry hall. Straight away she could smell musty dampness. She took off her coat and then her jumper, using it to rub her hair dry.

"Home sweet home," he said.

Not much of a home. The carpet must have been older than she was, worn and dirty, and the stairs were worse. No carpet there, just bare floorboards with an occasional nail sticking out. The walls must have been covered in picture frames once but all there was now were lots of square shadow outlines, ghosts of the pictures, against the awful zigzagged pattern of the 1970s wallpaper.

"This'll do nicely, we'll be right as rain here," he said, rubbing his hands together and walking towards the kitchen. "I'll get the kettle on and then we can start getting things ready."

She was going to ask him what they were getting ready for but she didn't bother. She knew anyway, or at least she knew what he thought they needed to get ready for. Supplies stored away. Be prepared for the end. She didn't have the energy for that. She knew she had to help him to stop thinking like this but she was wet through and her teeth were chattering, her makeup running as her hands trembled.

"Can I have any room?" "Either or," he called cheerily.

She climbed the stairs, the banister wobbling worryingly as she leant on it. Upstairs the damp smell was stronger. She looked in the bathroom and saw a greenish sink, greenish bath and no shower. She sighed and slammed the door shut. The first bedroom was tiny with just a single bed that might have been a child's bed, and a cream rug that had a large blue stain covering most of it. The second room was slightly bigger but it had a double bed. She coughed as she stepped inside, the mustiness taking her breath way.

"Well done, Dad," she said as she crossed the room, floorboards creaking, to open the window. But as her hand reached for the latch of the sash window she gave a small gasp. The windowsill was covered with dust and a few dead spiders but worse than that was the remains of a small bird lying on its back with its legs pointed up, most of it rotted away so it was really just a skeleton with a few feathers.

"Poor thing," she said, imagining it stuck somehow in the room, unable to get out. There were brownish marks on the window and she tried not to think of that, of it flying against the glass again and again. "How did you get stuck in here?"

Carefully she opened the window, the rain still

pouring down, but the fresh air and wind sweeping in and chasing the damp stench away. She thought of finding something to lift the bird with but there was nothing, so she gently lifted it by its feet and brought it to the window.

"There you go," she said. "I'm sorry."

She let go and the bird fell from her fingers, but instead of falling freely to the grass below, it became tangled with the creepers, its body finding a gap in the branches until it was stuck halfway down, trapped there.

The rain's spray was soaking her face. She tried to reach down and free the bird, shaking the creeper branches, but it wouldn't budge. It was truly stuck there, on its back again as it had been when she found it, in the branches like they were some ugly echo of its nest. She shook the branches again, harder, but it was no good. She stepped back and shut the window, slamming it down hard so the glass rattled. Her face was wet, her eyes were wet, and her body was trembling though she wasn't sure why. *I'm not sad, I'm not, it was dead already.* But still she trembled. She held out her arms, hands flat and palms up. She watched her hands tremble almost like they were a separate thing to her body and no matter how much she willed them to stop, they still trembled. It was the rain, the cold, she knew that, that was all, just the rain but even then, knowing that, her hands refused to listen.

"Rose Cottage," she said. "Rose." She kept saying the words over and over until eventually the trembling stopped and her hands were calm and the sound of the rain battering the world was ended.

Chapter Seven

There was a man and he wouldn't let go of her arm.

His beard was long and black, strands of ashes all matted and entangled, and his eyes as ash-black too but darker even, the very emptiest hollows of space. His nails dug into her arm as he pulled her towards him and she in turn scratched and hit his arm but no matter how hard she hit or how much she tried to pull herself, he wouldn't let go. She felt that if she kept pulling, she might snap. The standing stones were all around them, encircling them, and there were sounds too. Cries and calls of desperation, screams, a distant rumble and then a sudden flash, the clatter of steel. She was screaming too. *Let go of me, let go of me, let go of me.* But he wouldn't. His black eyes were looking at her but they were empty and she knew he didn't see her, just held her, so that slowly she was dragged closer, inevitably so. She could feel her feet, bare and cold, sink into the mud as he used all his weight and strength to bring her to him. Now she could smell him. It was a smell of meat and sweat, of smoke and blood, a bad smell. But as she was pulled closer, she saw his face and, though his eyes looked blankly at her, he wasn't as hideous as she had thought. Not a monster because there are no monsters, not truly, she knew that. He was young and handsome. He was sad. His lips moved and he spoke but the sounds around them suffocated his words. A horn blew. A child laughed. She stopped fighting. Still pulling her arm away but with less effort, less sureness that she had to free herself. *Let me go, let me go, let me go,* she cried but there was no strength in her words. Weak, she let herself be pulled towards him as his mouth moved and the silent words were spoken.

"What are you saying?" she shouted but his black eyes looked past her and her feet were caked in mud and the rain was falling.

She woke, sweating though the room was freezing because her dad hadn't been able to figure out the heating. She was dizzy too, sick. She sat up and reached for her cigarettes, lit one and smoked it. It didn't do much to chase away the sickliness inside her. She ran her hand over her forehead and felt the sweat there. She knew the dream had been bad but even now, just seconds after waking, it was already distant and becoming lost. All she knew was that she had been afraid and then not afraid. She smoked the cigarette too low to the filter and then smoked another. She showered, the water just about warm, and it was only when she got back to her room and looked at her phone, saw it was noon, did she realise how late she had slept. There was a message from Spencer.

Why've you gone on holiday?

She sat on her bed, shivering in her underwear, and replied.

I had to, Dad needed it. Be back soon. Still want to meet?

She opened her Instagram and went to Skan's page. She knew she should message him, tell him where they were, but she knew too he wouldn't reply. Had he really stopped caring about her? It didn't seem possible, to go away somewhere and be one person and then become someone else just because you had gone there. He even looked different. He had dyed his hair blonde and he had three piercings in his nose and a spike through his ear. The girl in the picture with him was sticking out her tongue and she had blue hair, a stud through her tongue. Skan was kissing her in the picture and Kyle wondered what the girl's name was. She had always thought that Skan would tell

103

her about any girls he met. He always used to tell her when he liked someone in his class.

"Promise me you won't tell," he would say and she would promise. *I promise.* It was silly, she knew that, there was no one she could've told but it had made her feel close to him, like they were connected in some way beyond just a normal brother and sister, like they were real friends and that he trusted her. But all that broke the minute he left for London. *Did I break it?* She scrolled through pictures of him on holiday in Amsterdam and in the bar he worked at and at a football game. He had always hated football but there he was with the girl at a QPR match, looking happier than he had ever looked when he was home. She threw her phone to her pillow and dressed.

Downstairs it was much colder so she took her duffel from the banister and put it on, hugging her arms about herself, keeping her hands hidden within the sleeves. The TV was on in the living room and her dad was asleep in the chair. Same as ever. She moved quietly into the living room and looked at him. The TV was on to BBC news so she knew he had been up all night, watching, waiting for those tiny confirmations, the hints of truth or those innocent facts that he would shape towards his truth.

"What do I do, Dad?" she whispered.

There was a glass of whisky on the table and he

was still wearing the same clothes he had on when they had left home. Then he had looked smart and changed, like the clothes were hope. Maybe that was just all in her head. *My hope.* Now the shirt was untucked and there was a stain from dinner on his trousers. He was a mess again but she had no idea how to fix him. She looked around the living room. It wasn't home but it might as well have been. His notebooks were on the other couch and there was no one there but the two of them. *Nothing changes if you stay in the same place.* She picked up the whisky and sniffed it. It smelled strong. She took a sip and the heat of the liquid warmed her body, so she drank the rest, her throat burning, screwing her eyes up as she swallowed. She reached for the remote and turned off the TV.

Here doesn't have to be the same, not if I make it different.

She knew what to do. At home they would eat ready meals and never see each other; she would be in her room and he would be in his with all the confusion of the internet to break his mind.

"You have to start small," Skan used to say when he was getting up at five every day to do his paper round. "You can't just have what you want without knowing how to get it."

She knew what she wanted. She wanted her dad

well again and normal. Small steps. She would take small steps like cooking him a meal and sitting with him, watching a film, talking to him. Small steps. She went into the kitchen. The shopping bags were still unpacked but there was nothing good to eat, just tins of beans, macaroni and ravioli. In the dining room there was a long table with three chairs. Oddly, there was an old bike leaning against the wall that looked like nobody had ridden it for years, out of place and without use. The idea came then, obvious and simple. All she had to do was ride into the town to buy some things to cook and that would be the first small step to making him well. Small wheels.

She pulled the bike away from the wall and tested the thin wheels. They were stiff but it wasn't as bad or as locked up with age as she had first feared. There was even a basket on the front where she could put the shopping. She smiled as she dinged the little bell on the handlebar and turned the bike away from where it had been abandoned, forgotten, for too long. As she wheeled it out of the room she noticed a framed photograph on the mantelpiece. She leant the bike carefully back against the wall. The photograph was small, especially in its overlarge frame. It was old, older than the bike even, yellowed. It showed the cottage but it wasn't as creeper-covered or derelict. There were flowers in the garden, roses, and standing in front of the house was a family. There was a tall man, big and broad, slightly overweight, with precisely parted hair and round glasses. He was holding hands with a small woman, delicate and thin in a summer dress. In front of her was a boy of around eleven who was holding a fat tabby cat in his arms and there was another cat on the windowsill, black as ashes, sleeping in the sun. A black and tan mongrel dog was sitting on the doorstep and on the grass, cross- legged, was a little girl of four or five with tight curly hair, holding one hand up as if she was waving. They all looked so happy, like they were in the happiest place in the world. *See, if a place has been happy once it can be happy again.* Small steps.

She wheeled the bike along the hall, her dad still sleeping silently, his chest rising and falling steadily, and opened the door. There on the doorstep was a rabbit.

She stopped. The rabbit was on its back, legs stretched out. There was a little red hole in its head and she knew it was dead. That was all there was, just a dead rabbit with no note or explanation. She stared at it for a moment, trying her best to fight away the niggling thought that this was somehow some kind of bad sign to shatter the hope she had forced herself to find. But it was just a rabbit, she knew that. Just a rabbit.

She pushed the bike past the rabbit and rode down the sloping road towards the big house. It was as cold as it had been all week but the rain had stopped and she could hear the sea, the gentle wash coming from her right where the cliffs stood not far away. The air felt good against her groggy body and the sickliness started to lessen. The road curved to her right and then began to climb again towards the house. She peddled harder, the seat firm and bony against her bottom, so she lifted herself a little away from it and rode like she would when she was younger, almost standing as she peddled harder and harder to climb the steepening hill. At the top was the grand house but now in the clarity of the rainless day she saw it was as dilapidated and unloved as the cottage, not nearly as grand as she had imagined it must be. The windows were dirty and the curtains were threadbare, old. There was a plant, almost the beginnings of a tree, growing out of the gutters, and the roof had more tiles missing than tiles left.

She didn't notice the old woman until she was practically riding into her. She was sat in a fold-out chair in the middle of the road, looking up at the roof, one hand shading her eyes against the midday sun. She was still wearing her nighty and her swollen purplish legs were bare despite the chill. Kyle had to swerve quickly around her.

"Sorry," Kyle called, glancing back, but the woman hadn't moved. Her hand was still shielding her eyes and she was still looking up to the roof as if Kyle had never been there.

Kyle rode on. The road flattened out now and the cold air was welcome against her body as she peddled faster and faster, waking her and reviving her. She found herself smiling again as she whizzed along the road, past the moors and down towards the town. Out on the moor she saw wild horses, all grazing. She brought the bike to a stop and took a breath. Most of the horses were quietly eating grass, lost in their own simple thoughts. But there was one, a large stallion, muscular and stern-eyed. His head was held high and he was looking out towards the east, just staring. Kyle looked too. The sky wasn't so clear that way, more clouds bringing more snow or rain for the evening, tinged a little with red. She took a picture of him and uploaded it to her Instagram.

There were rabbits too. She had never seen so many rabbits. Rabbits in the road so she had to zigzag through them, rabbits at the roadside, rabbits on the moor sat between the legs of a horse, rabbits watching her as she raced by.

When she finally reached St Christopher she was breathing hard, her heart racing, but it felt good for it to beat with such pace. She couldn't remember the last time her heart had beat so fast. The road dipped now so she stopped pedaling hard, letting the bike freewheel the rest of the way into town. No cars passed by. A bus was ahead of her but as she neared it, she simply tilted the handlebars and curved smoothly around.

The cobbles of the quayside road bumped her the final way into town and, beaming happily, she got off the bike and rolled it towards the post office. There was nowhere to lock it but she had no lock anyway, so she leant it against a post box and went inside. She bought two packets of twenty Marlboro and the owner didn't even ask her for ID.

"Do you have any fudge?" she asked because it was her dad's favourite.

"Devon or Cornish?" said the grim-looking owner. He was grey-haired and his face was a little grey too. He looked sort of seasick, jowly and bored as he weighed out the Devon fudge.

Kyle bought *The Mirror* and *The Guardian*. She glanced over the front page of *The Mirror* as the owner added up what she owed. The headline said "Storm Warning". There was a collage of photographs: a submarine, Putin, the President, the Belgian nightclub that was attacked, the Muslim man who did it, a Russian soldier, a hand, reaching out across the sand of a beach, limp and lifeless, the MP who was killed in Ipswich last week, a group of politicians sat around a shiny table, a protest in Madrid. She folded the paper up and smiled widely to the owner as she took her change.

"Thank you," she sang as she left the shop.

She walked up and down the high street, trying to think of something to cook. The butchers seemed to specialise solely in sausages but she hadn't eaten sausages since Year Eight because of the pigs her school had adopted. All she really knew to cook was lasagne like her gran had taught her, so she kept walking in search of a Tesco or deli where she could buy the ingredients. She tried to remember all the ingredients she would need, hoping she had enough money. *Lasagne sheets, mince, white sauce, garlic, tomatoes, onions, carrots, cheese.* As she neared the Checky Cat, she saw the boy from the bus stop crossing the street and ducking through the low pub door. She remembered his backpack full of rabbits and the rabbit on her doorstep, and without thinking she marched quicker and followed him in.

The pub was small and dark, the ceiling low with black beams. Immediately she regretted going in. There were only men in the pub. One sat at the bar, leaning into a pint, the barman tipping a pint glass to a tap and pulling a pump as beer flowed into the glass, and an old man with a scabby-haired collie dog sat a table looking up at the horse racing. There were posters of football teams on the wall, Celtic and Liverpool, and some old Guinness plaques. At the far end of the bar on its own stool sat a stuffed, striped cat, its dirty fur pink and white.

She was about to turn away when the boy appeared out of a side door, fastening his belt. He saw her and grinned, one too fair eyebrow arching.

"Alright there, you. Didn't expect to see you here."

She wanted to turn away and go straight back out, but instead she held the plastic bag with the newspapers in close to her and stayed.

"I wanted a drink," she said, trying to sound sure that was why she had really come in. He grinned wider. "Did you now? No better place to come for one."

He shook his head and went to the bar and took the beer. "Can she have one, Russ?" The barman looked over at her and scratched his stubble.

"Don't see why not," he said gummily. "You're havin' one aren't you."

"I am," said the boy and he turned to her. "What'll it be?"

She had never been in a pub, not by herself or without her dad. She had never even asked for a drink other than coke before and when she drank with her friends it was only ever cheap cider or straight vodka.

"Vodka and coke," she said, hearing her own voice small and young in the dank pub.

The man with the dog glanced up at her and shook his head. "You have a seat," said the boy. "I'll bring it over."

She looked around. There was a booth at the far end tucked tightly into a curved alcove, a bench on either side, so she sat there. She took off her coat and bit her fingernail, wondered what her dad would say if he knew she was in a pub. Really, she doubted he would be angry but it wasn't fear of that which bothered her. *I'm here for Dad, to help him.* But instead of that she was in a pub with a strange boy without a single ingredient to make lasagne.

"There you go," said the boy putting her glass down and squeezing into the other side of the booth. He was big, far too big, bulky and awkward. His legs knocked the table so she had to grab her glass to stop it spilling as he squeezed in, and he had to lean forward so his head didn't touch the low curved ceiling. He took a book from his coat pocket as he made himself comfortable and laid it on the table.

"Good spot," he said. "Sorry, I..."

"...never been in a pub before," he said, finishing her sentence. "That's not what I was going to say."

"I know that. Do you remember my name?"

She took a sip of her drink and tasted the cheap coke and strong vodka and wondered if he'd ordered her a double.

"No," she said but she did remember. Cerys always said when you like a boy you should never let on you like him. Never let him know that you care anything about him. She took another sip. *But I don't like him.* His face was too wide and pale, the strange cross scar on his cheek that she couldn't figure out how he got, and the way he looked at her, even now, like he was eating her, drinking her, consuming her.

"Isaac," he said, making the name sound flat and everyday. "Isaac Marcaret. I reckon I told you that."

"I wasn't listening," she said, more coldly than she'd meant to and then the memory of the dead rabbit returned, and the words tumbled out angrily. "Did you leave a rabbit on my doorstep?"

He grinned again and winked at her. His teeth were as white as his hair. "I might have."

She frowned at his bravado. "Don't you think that's a bit weird? Leaving dead rabbits on people's doorsteps. I mean did you follow me or something?"

He laughed and took a large gulp of his beer. "Why would I do that?"

He waited for her to answer but she only looked away. The man at the bar had his head to the bar and

114

the barman was pouring a double rum from an optic which he then drank in one go.

"I wouldn't follow you, don't worry about that," said Isaac. "I knew you were staying there, that's all."

She looked back at him. Her hand went to the bag, ready to leave.

He sat back, moving the huge frame of his body away. It was a shadow, large and dominating in the small space, but as she shuffled back, she felt like she could breathe a little better. "Don't get nervous or that, I'm not a stalker. My mam owns the big house and the cottage. My family owns lots of land on the island. Grandad used to say we owned most of Selny when it came down to it, or at least we did, anyway, till Dad died and Mam started selling everything. I live in the big house too. I knew when I saw you in town that you were the ones staying there. Halfpenny isn't it?"

She let go of the bag. "Yeah. Halfpenny." "Do you have a first name?"

She bit her nail again and then stopped herself, remembering that he was looking at her, studying her. "Kyle."

He laughed. It wasn't a cruel laugh. "Why you got a boy's name?" "It's not a boy's name, it's a girl's name. It's my name."

He laughed again and took another gulp of beer.

115

"Alright then, it's a girl's name. I believe you." He took another drink, longer. She looked at his rough stubble and wondered how old he was. "I like it," he said and then like he could read her thoughts, added, "how old are you anyway? Sixteen?"

She shook her head. "More like fifteen."
"Shouldn't be in here then."

Her leg was moving slightly under the table, one foot tapping against her ankle. "Should you be in here?"

He shrugged, his big shoulders hunching. "Maybe. Depends who's serving. If it's Russ then yeah, if Benny then probably not. Maybe another year and it won't matter who's serving."

He drained the last of his pint and motioned with the glass to the door. "I saw one of them Arabs getting off the ferry. What do you reckon to that?"

Her foot tapped faster. "What do you mean?"

"Just thinking what with all the immigrants and that, I was thinking are they coming here now. You know, gypsies and Arabs and all that."

"You can't say things like that," she said, sitting back too quickly so her head banged against the bare stone wall. Ignoring the pain she waited for him to apologise but he only grinned.

"I can say what I want. Who's it going to hurt?"

"People," she said. She took another drink. The

vodka was so strong she was starting to wonder if he had given her a treble. She wanted to tell him he was stupid, a big lump of stupid, that nobody talked like that about people, not good people, not clever people, but she only swallowed the vodka and shook her head in disgust. "How would you like it if people talked about you just because of where you were born"?

"Wouldn't bother me. People all think things in their heads, no knowing what the person next to you is thinking so why worry. Worry like that sends a person off their head." His eyes looked down to her bare arms so she pulled them away, placing them on her legs beneath the table.

"You shouldn't think like that. Everyone is just everyone."

"That's fine if you come from where you do, but Selny, it's not as big as England. We get a boat full of them lot and that's the whole population doubled. That can't be right."

She had heard boys speak like that before. Boys in her class and boys in town. Men too. Her dad's friends, a couple at the bus stop as an Asian woman passed. The word they shouted. The fear. She had never felt that sort of fear but she never knew how to tell those who did just how wrong they were. Everyone is just everyone, that was how a teacher had put it but when she said it to Isaac she hardly knew what it meant and it didn't seem to say what she wanted. *Everyone should be able to be anyone.*

"Another?" he said.

She knew she should say no. That she should go, buy the ingredients and ride home as quickly as possible and never speak or think of Isaac Marcaret again. Bury the poor rabbit and forget all about the boy. But instead she found herself nodding.

"Rebel," he said and as he stood, his long legs hit the table and his head nodded against the ceiling so his waxed flat hair was messed up. He was still bending over as he made his way to the bar, his huge body aware of the smallness of the space around him.

Her foot still tapping, she finished her drink and waited. The confusing words of the horse racing commentary came to her like muffled conversations, indistinct and distant. The pub smelled stale with an overpowering whiff of fishiness whose origin she didn't want to think too much about. She wondered if she could go back right then, just run out and not worry about him calling after her or whether he would turn up at the cottage with more rabbits. Just go. Just ignore whatever it was that was making her stay, and go.

But she stayed.

Searching for something to do to stop her mind from turning itself over and over with doubt, she reached across the table and shifted the book around so it was facing her. It was a hardback like you hardly ever saw anymore and the cover was worn here and there like old parchment. It looked like it came from another time, long ago. The cover was light blue, like Isaac's strange eyes, and in old fashioned, faded black the author's name was printed across the top. *Jonezy Maw.* Beneath that was a simple linocut drawing of a fox, outlined in black and coloured in white. Curving around the fox was the title. *The Pale Fox.* She was about to open it to the first page when Isaac arrived back with the drinks and just about squeezed himself into the small gap between table, bench and wall.

"You read it before?" he said, placing her drink clumsily down.

"Never," she said, her hand still on the book, the crinkled cover feeling somehow reassuring against her palm. "I don't really read much."

The racing commentary grew louder. Excited calls of horses' names and the roar of an equally excited crowd. "Me neither. 'Bout the only book I ever have read." He coughed, clearing his throat. *"Far away, beyond the confines of his life, there was a war. Not a war that you or I would ever read about in the evening paper. Not a war we might hear rumours of as we settled in for an evening around the wireless with our loved ones. Not a war that most of us, nearly all of us, were ever meant* to see or hear or know of. But a war all the same and one whose limits and goals stretched beyond the prison of its own world and sought to reach out, break through into our world and make us see it, hear it, know of it. For, just there beyond the edge of the known there has ever been another place, a shadow place, a world within a world. Those who know of it call it Marorn and those who do not know of it might believe it to be a dream, a story, a fable. The Jarsdel children had always been fond of stories..."

His voice changed as he spoke. Not so rough, not so hard. It was practised and precise, not struggling or stumbling over words, clean and confidently he recited them from memory.

"Is that from this?" she said and he nodded.

His voice returned to its coarseness. "Couldn't read when my dad got me this. I was about ten. Now I can read but I only read this." He learned forward and looked her in her eyes like he wanted to tell her a secret, the table wobbling. "It's true, you know. There is another world, I've seen it."

There was a certainty to his voice now that didn't come from something written down or rehearsed, even back in its own rough cage, one she had heard before. Her dad's certainty. She looked down at her glass, took a breath and then looked up to his eyes. She knew what that illness looked like and without knowing why, she hoped she wouldn't see it there. And so she didn't. His eyes were the same as they had been, crystal-blue and strange but not sick. Just certain.

"What do you mean?" she said, her voice soft, quiet.

He shuffled uneasily in his seat and she wasn't sure if that was for lack of comfort or with nerves for what he was letting her in on. "Like Marorn in the book. I've seen it for myself on the moors at night. The horses, they get spooked and when they get to running you can see them, the Riders, not just horses but men too. It's like they're only half there and when you go up near the stones you can feel it, something dragging on you, pulling on you even though you know you shouldn't let it."

His words trailed off and he sat back against the stone wall, looked down at his pint. "Maybe, anyway. At least, I think sometimes it all be might be real."

Kyle looked at the book. She traced her finger around the outline of the fox. "What is it?" she asked. "I mean the fox. What is it in the book?"

He glanced up, his brow set heavy and guarded. "It's a fox." He was closed up now, she recognised that. He'd said too much, given too much of himself and now he was falling back in, building the walls. Private Property.

"I know that," she said, smiling, trying to put him at ease. "But why"?

He frowned, trying to puzzle out whether she might make fun of him and then he relaxed and grinned. "There's a fox, pale as a ghost it is. Thing is, if you see it, like Jonas does in the book, it means you'll know death, no escaping that, you'll know it in some way."

"Know it?"

He nodded. "Know it. Like you'll face it, like Jonas does. It's not Maw's story, she just used it for the book. It's an old Selny story, all of it is. My grandad told me even Marorn is just the old name for the island, that when he was a kid they used to say beware the white fox, watch out for Riders on the moors, that witches built the stones and all that. Stories like that, like the pale fox, they're old aren't they? They don't go away and then someone uses them for a story and everyone thinks they're not real. What I always think is how the story started; people just don't make stuff like that up. Nah, it's real, all of it is. Stands to reason it is."

They were quiet for a while. He took long sups and she took short ones. The vodka wasn't so strong this time but it was making her tired, drowsy, and all she could think about was the ride home and the meal she had promised herself she would make for her dad. She ran over the ingredients she would need again in her head. *Lasagne sheets, mince, white sauce, garlic, tomatoes, onions, carrots, cheese.* Kept saying them to herself so they'd stick.

"You here long?" he said at last, a little nervously still. "Not too long. A week or so."

He leant forward, his habit of filling a space, and pushed the book over to her, too roughly though she could tell he never meant to. All of him just seemed pre-programmed to that, to roughness.

"You can take it, though you'll have to promise to give it me back. It's my only copy."

She shook her head. "I can't take it, it's yours."

"Course you can. Even for a day, I don't mind. You might like it anyway."

She looked down to the book, his hand still on it, holding it in place so she couldn't refuse it.

"Take it," he said. "Maybe meet me tomorrow afternoon and I'll take you up to the stones. I could show you the rabbits too, show you how I hunt them. You can give me it back then if you like."

She didn't say anything. His hand was big, his fingers wide and fingernails dirty at the edges. There was a cut along his index finger, nearly healed but it must have been deep when it happened.

"One day," she said, taking the book and placing it in the plastic bag with the newspapers.

"And you'll meet me tomorrow?"

She didn't look at him, looked instead to the bar

123

where the drunk was still sleeping and the noise of the horse racing was gone. She remembered Cerys' advice. Never let them know.

"Maybe," she said. She stood up and quickly she squeezed out of the booth and, without looking back at him, she hurried out of the pub into the too-bright afternoon, the fresh air and sudden light hitting her hard and making her head spin a little. She lit a cigarette but after one drag she tossed it away. The lasagne ingredients were jumbled now. *Lasagne sheets, mince, garlic, tomatoes, onions, carrots, cheese.* She knew she was forgetting something as she followed the street around away from the quay and found a Co-op. At the till she still couldn't remember what the last ingredient was and fumbled her money to the checkout boy. It was only when she rode the bike heavily home, leaning left then right, as she passed where the wild horses had been but were now gone, that she remembered the white sauce.

Chapter Eight

It was past midnight but she couldn't sleep. She
had been messaging Spencer, back and forth, but
every time she waited for his reply her mind would
wander to Isaac and then, when Spencer's reply came
through, she would have this tiny disappointment
right down in her stomach that it wasn't Isaac who
she was messaging. Soon, Spencer's talk of music
and Rose's funeral and old films began to bore her
and she lay back on the bed and closed her eyes.
Straight away, like it was just waiting there for her to
find space, she thought of Isaac. She could feel the
hard edges of his voice, harsh and uncaring of what
anyone thought. No, not hear it. Just feel it, like it
had imprinted on her, like all his bulk taking up all
that space in the booth had left some mark on her
that wouldn't shift. She didn't mind it. She could see

him now, a vague and tall figure, pale and blonde, large hands reaching out to touch her face, and she imagined asking him how he got the scar.

"This?" he said, touching his cheek. "Oh, I was born with this."

She opened her eyes. Outside the rain was a constant wash against the flimsy protection of the window, rivers and streams confused in their overlapping upon the pane. From downstairs she could just make out the sound of the television, the steady and monotonous tones of the news. She turned on her side, brought her legs up close to her chest. Her phone buzzed but she ignored it. Dinner had been a disaster. She had known it would be as soon as she got home, sweating and exhausted. He had been drinking again, still sat in the same chair but with a half empty bottle of Jameson's on the table, a notebook on his lap and crumpled up scraps of paper strewn about the floor.

"I'm cooking tea," she had announced, trying to sound cheery even though she wanted to run upstairs and be alone.

Without looking up from his writing he grunted, "That's lovely."

The lasagne wasn't lovely and nor was it a lasagne, not really. There was some flour in the cupboard, browner than the flour she was used to. She had

126

hoped that wasn't because it was twenty years past
its use-by. She had tried to make a white sauce with
the UHT milk but the lumps wouldn't go away and it
tasted bitter. She hadn't used it in the end and when
the lasagne came out of the oven the sheets were
more burnt than deliciously crispy, and the whole
thing had shrunk in on itself, like it was trying to
hide from its own failings. Still trying to make things
good, she had suggested they eat at the dining room
table.

"You can't stay there all day," she had said, tiredly,
the will for what she had known so certainly and
hopefully she would do all leaking away.

"I'm good here, love," he had said and so they
ate in silence while he watched the news. She could
think of nothing to say, no words to motivate him or
to pull him from the edge he was tottering over. She
felt heavy, and the lasagne, so shrivelled and sweet
with tomatoes, took away any appetite she had left.

"Kyle," he had said, as *Pointless* ended and the news
began. She shivered a little at what might be coming.
He was calling her to listen, to hear something of
utter importance. She could hear that in how he
said her name. *Kyle*. He made her name sound too
full of weight, sinking, drowning. "I know this must
be difficult for you, being here, but when you think
about it this is a good thing." He paused, waiting for

her to respond. To give him affirmation. She kept her eyes locked on the disappointing meal, the shrivelled pasta, the dried sauce. When she said nothing he sighed and went on. "This is a good place for us to start again, Kyle. We're stronger than anyone else, you and I, stronger than the world knows."

She dug her fork into a piece of lasagne but didn't lift it to her mouth. "What if you're wrong," she said, still not looking at him. "Will we go back then?"

She heard his fork clatter against his plate. "Kyle," he said and there it was again, the ruining of her name, the weight it didn't ask for. "There's no escaping what's coming but Christ I promise you I will keep you safe, nothing could ever stop me from keeping you safe. I'm sorry, but this is all there is now, you and I and this place. No, love, we're never going back home. This is home now."

And so it all broke and shattered like it was always going to break and shatter. There was no sound to the breaking, the opposite. Just silence. Just the space between them filling with an ugly silence and her realisation, as heavy as the weight he gave her name, that he was gone, too far gone for her to bring him back. *I promise.* She hated promises.

The evening news began.

"Look at this," her dad said between mouthfuls, pointing at the television. He turned it up louder so the Welsh newsreader was almost shouting his report.

"…Russia has warned NATO that any further incidents will be seen as acts of aggression and all necessary steps will be taken to respond…"

She stopped listening. Pushed her fork around her plate, cut a hard piece of lasagne in half and brought it reluctantly to her mouth then brought it back to the plate. While she cleaned the dishes he stayed in the living room, drinking and writing, and she looked past her own reflection in the sheen of the window to the rain and the night. When the dishes were stacked neatly away she passed the living room without saying a word and climbed the stairs to her room. There was a war, she knew that, and it was the war for her dad's mind, for the return of who had been. It was a war she was losing, a war that she might have already lost.

In bed she rolled over to her side and reached out to switch the lamp on. The light was harsh so she screwed up her eyes. On her bedside table were the two books, the one her gran had given her and Isaac's. She sat up, pushing the pillows up behind her, and lifted *The Eagle of the Ninth*. She could vaguely remember the story, about a Roman centurion and a slave boy, but even as she held the book it was Skan's voice that she associated with it, no one else's. The story hadn't mattered, it was Skan being next to her, reading to her until sleep came that had mattered. She flipped past her mother's name to the first page but the words were empty to her. She read them once and then once again but they wouldn't go in. Her voice, the voice she heard in her head while she read, was not Skan's voice. Skan's voice was far away. It was becoming a struggle to remember it clearly. It was there, in the safest part of her mind, but it was foggy and distant. One day, she knew, she would forget that voice and that time when it was just the two of them together.

She dropped the book to the bed and lifted *The Pale Fox* but she knew even before she opened it that she had no will to read. Words, they were becoming so hard to concentrate on. Even at school, her coursework and the knowledge her teachers were cramming her full of before the exams next year were difficult to hold on to. She had always been near the top of her class, not the brightest but near enough to never feel pressure, and yet lately nothing stayed. By the end of a school day she would forget what she had just learned in last period and when it came to revision she would stare blankly at the books, not able to read past one paragraph without turning to her phone or switching the TV back on. She felt a cliché of her age but, despite knowing that, the problem only got worse.

The white fox waited for her patiently to start reading but she let the book fall to join *The Eagle of the Ninth* and picked up her phone. The message from Spencer flashed insistently but she ignored it, opened the internet and typed in *The Pale Fox*. The first hit was for Wikipedia and she opened that. Beside all the writing and information was a black and white photograph of a pretty young woman with short hair, a severe fringe, straight. Kyle clicked on the Jonezy Maw link.

Jonezy Maw

From Wikipedia, the free encyclopaedia

Joan 'Jonezy' de Montfort Maw (6 December 1912 – 23 July 1947) *was an English novelist best known for children's books, especially retellings of Manx and Selnic myths and legends. Her only novel,* The Pale Fox, *was published after her death and is often voted amongst the greatest children's novels of the twentieth century. Maw was the daughter of the MP, Charles Kintore Maw and the French actress Sandrine de Montfort. She died of tuberculosis in Paris in the summer of 1947, two years before* The Pale Fox *found publication with Hutter, Hutter & Stack with the now classic illustrations by the Austrian surrealist Imanol Uberschar.*

Kyle lingered over the photograph of Maw. The young woman was smiling, her eyes bright and happy.

The photograph was dated 1945, two years before her death. There didn't look an ounce of sickness in her, just happiness.

She flicked back to *The Pale Fox* wiki-page. *I won't meet him,* she had told herself as she rode the bike home, *I promise I won't meet him.* But now, as she skimmed the plot, scrolling down the screen, she knew she was doing it so they would have something to talk about. She knew she would go back to the Checky Cat tomorrow.

In the winter of 1935, five siblings – Jonas, Astrid, Beckett, Lionel and Esther Jarsdel – are sent to stay with their father's sister on the island of Selny while their mother recuperates from a long illness. Once on Selny, the siblings begin to explore the island, looking for adventures to pass the time. They meet an old farmer, Rumsbrigg, who tells them the story of a fox that can pass between our world and another world that the old farmer calls Marorn. He warns the children not to go near the Penny Stones but, spurred on by boredom and the possibility of more adventures, the children ignore his warnings and play amongst the stones. When Astrid jumps on to the Sun Stone there is a sudden flash and she vanishes. Perplexed, the other siblings decide that they have to climb the Sun Stone too in the hope of finding their sister. Holding hands, they climb on top of the high stone and wait. Just as the youngest boy, Lionel, announces that Esther was playing a trick on them, there is a second flash and the siblings are thrown into another world.

Astrid, going through first, finds herself in a ruined castle on top of a hill. There is a plinth with a shining jewel on top and she is inexplicably drawn to it. Upon touching it she begins to change, her skin turning icy blue and her eyes black. She collapses.

Meanwhile, the four other Jarsdel siblings are thrown into the middle of a battle between Prince Cadric and his brother Kevarl. Kevarl is a servant of the demon Obrax and is being driven to destroy Marorn and find a way to the 'new world' where Obrax can feed on new souls. Protecting his younger siblings, Jonas finds himself face to face with Kevarl. He picks up a sword and stands his ground as Kevarl attacks. In the distance beyond Kevarl, Jonas sees a fox running across the battlefield. The fox is white as a ghost. Just as the dark prince brings down his axe, Cadric steps in the way and is slain. A horn blows and the Riders of Marorn thunder towards the battle, sweeping away Kevarl's evil forces of stonesouls, runemages, wargfolk and skrye.

Injured, Jonas is carried back to the city of Ginadrin, where he and his siblings are told only those of the World Beyond can defeat Kevarl but Kevarl seeks their power too. Obrax has given Kevarl a Corrim, a jewel that can absorb the energy of Beyonders and open a portal into our world through which Obrax means to pass.

At Ginadrin, the witch Ramor gives the Jarsdel children each a gift or power. To Jonas she gives the strongest gift, the power to slay the work of demons with a red-bladed sword.

Meanwhile, Astrid wakes in a bed chamber. Obrax is there in the form of a handsome young man. The blue has drained from Astrid but the black remains in her eyes. Astrid is seduced by Obrax into telling him about her siblings. Astrid falls in love with the demon and when they kiss she is forever connected to Marorn.

The other Jarsdel children are guided by the pig squire Paddershore and the troll Kedmick, across the demon-infested west of the island to Kevarl's castle of Skurran. There they must destroy the Corrim before Kevarl can use it to drain their powers. But before they reach the castle, they are ambushed and Jonas is separated from his siblings. In a forest, he is pursued by Kevarl until the two meet in a clearing. Kevarl tells him he too has seen the Pale Fox and wonders which one of them will know death first. They fight and it is only when Kevarl slips on a root that Jonas is able to kill him. With his last words, Kevarl reminds Jonas that he too will soon know death. Kevarl tells him that he was only trying to protect his world, not destroy it, and that he meant only to use Obrax to make Marorn stronger.

The Riders and the Low Folk attack Skurran while Beckett, Lionel and Esther find their way through the

Undertunnels up into Obrax's throne room. There they find Astrid, sitting on a throne dressed as Obrax's queen. Revealed in his true form, Obrax mocks the children and begins to use the Corrim to drain their power, but at the last moment, Jonas arrives and destroys the Corrim with his red blade. The power of the Corrim was all that was keeping Obrax alive and so he dies with it. His spell over Astrid is broken and she awakes from her trance.

Returning to Ginadrin, the siblings ask Ramor to help them return home, but the witch reveals that a great wound has been done to both worlds and that Obrax's evil has almost destroyed both. For the worlds to remain separate and safe, one of the Beyonders must remain in Marorn and as Astrid is connected to the world, she volunteers. Ramor tells the siblings that no one but them will remember Astrid in their world and that they, to enable the worlds to remain safe, will never be able to return to Marorn.

Saying their farewells to their sister, the other Jarsdel siblings return to the standing stone where Ramor and her witch sisters use their power to open a portal. When they arrive back at their aunt's house nobody asks about Astrid but a telegram has come from London.

To my four angels, I am well. Mamma.

Years later, Jonas is fighting in Germany towards the end of the Second World War. As he crosses a field, he sees the Pale Fox for a second time. He realises that the *fox can pass between both worlds and knows that his time is coming soon but he is happy because he knows he has helped protect his world, both in Marorn and in the War. As German parachutes descend, he runs into a forest to meet his fate.*

Kyle frowned, looking to the little book on her bed. She wondered how such a small book could be so full of sadness. It wasn't a happy story, not one bit, and she couldn't understand why Isaac kept going back to it over and over if he knew it ended in such a way. Books were meant to take you away from how cruel and rubbish the world could be, not remind you of it. *Why would anyone want to read about such sad things? Poor Astrid.*

She put on her dressing gown and took her cigarettes and lighter from her coat pocket. Carefully, trying without much success to stop the floorboards from creaking, she made her way downstairs and into the kitchen. It was raining still but there was an old gazebo at the end of the garden. She put on her dad's trainers and opening the door, she took a deep breath and ran as fast as she could across the sodden grass. Mud squelched and splashed and splattered all up her legs, the icy air rushing into her lungs and her dressing gown soaked through within a few steps. Breathless, she reached the shelter and lit a cigarette. For a while she smoked and watched the rain fall.

In the distance she could hear the faint rumble of thunder. When she was done smoking she took out her phone. It was late, she knew that, but her fingers tapped to her mum's number and she pressed dial. It rang as always and she expected it to keep ringing just the same as always but after four rings somebody answered.

"Hello," said a woman's voice, just woken and uncertain.

Kyle was frozen. She tried to speak but only a strange squeak came out.

"Who's this?" said the voice, groggily. A dog barked in the background. "Hello?"

Kyle cleared her throat. The rain hammered the gazebo roof, her body cold within the wet-through gown. "Hello," she managed to say, barely a whisper.

"Who's that?" said the voice, now angrier as the speaker woke. "Do you know what time it is?"

The voice wasn't familiar at all but then Kyle could hardly remember what her mum's real voice sounded like. Sometimes she would close her eyes and try to remember but if any voice came she knew it wasn't quite right. This woman's voice sounded just like those imagined voices. It wasn't soft. It wasn't kind. It wasn't what a mother's voice should sound like.

"Mum," she said, a croak.

There was silence. The dog kept barking, a little

yapping bark of some kind of terrier. "Mum. It's me, it's Kyle."

Still just the barking dog and the woman breathing.

"I'm sorry," said the woman, her voice quivering. "I think you've got the wrong number. Goodbye."

And before Kyle could say another word the line went dead. Her whole body went limp, collapsing back against the gazebo. She was crying now, crying like she hadn't cried in all her life, shaking and crying, and she put her arms about the gazebo and held tight as she cried. Suddenly there was a loud boom and then a whoosh of air and the ground seemed to shake. The shock of the sound stopped her tears and she looked up, face soaked, to the night and saw a flash of light amidst the clouds. A sonic boom: she had heard one before. Or at least that was what she thought it had been. Whatever it was, the light of it was gone and the sound of it too and there was only the rain and her own ragged breaths as she tried to calm herself.

She tapped her phone and brought up Skan's number, pressing dial before she could stop herself. It had been so long since they had spoken but all she wanted in the world right then was to hear his voice and tell him what had just happened. Maybe, wherever he was, he would answer and as they spoke, as he calmed her, she would hear the sonic boom as if the jet had just reached where he was and they would laugh together. The world wasn't such a big place. The phone rang.

When it answered it wasn't Skan's voice. "What?" said a woman sharply.

"Is Skan there?"

"What you want, bitch?" She was foreign, Eastern European. She would have sounded young if her voice wasn't so full of an anger that aged it, crippled it. "You think you ring here and talk to my boyfriend, slut? Huh, is that what you do? Ring him and tell him to come to you every day? Is that what you do, slut?"

The words were stuck in Kyle's throat, the tears back and rolling unstoppably down her cheeks. No one had ever spoken to her like that, spat such ugly words at her. Sharp bullets. She was trembling, one hand still gripping the gazebo though it did no good. She felt like she might fall off the world if she let go and yet the biggest part of her wanted to let go.

"No, that's not right," she managed to say, pleaded. "Tell him it's me, Kyle. I need him."

The girl laughed cruelly. "You need him, yeah. Well, he don't need you anymore, he had you already. Go away, bitch."

The phone went dead. Kyle let her arm drop to

her side and released her grip from the gazebo with the other. She didn't fall from the edge of the world. There was no edge. There was only this place like there was only ever this place, the same wherever she was. She stayed there in the gazebo, shaking and crying, her hands fumbling in the pocket of her dressing gown for her cigarettes and lighter. She flicked the lighter three times but no flame came. With a desperate scream she threw it out into the dark onto the rain- drowned grass and tossed the cigarette after it. She screamed again, louder, stronger, and then again and again until her body was emptied of any sound.

The call that answered was almost a yelp, a strange bark. She stepped down from the gazebo to the muddy grass and the sound came again. Her hair was drenched, plastered to her face, but she didn't run for the house. She peered into the dark of the garden. The sound came again. When eventually she saw what made the sound, it was just two points of light in the dark but she knew what it was. She couldn't see its body or colouring but she knew without a doubt that it was a fox and it was white as a ghost. She knew too what ending the fox's appearance would bring. She thought of her dad, passed out in the living room like always and the hard truth that there was and always had been nothing she could do to save him.

Hope can die. The rain fell on. The yelp came again and then, as if a light was being switched off, the fox turned its head and was gone.

Chapter Nine

The mirror showed her a worried face and a silver owl.

The delicate silver links of the necklace felt more than its slight weight against the skin of her neck. Unfamiliar, the owl with its jet eyes pressed down against her collar bone. She touched her hand to the clasp at the nape of her neck, then moved it away. She saw her face again, worried, the eyes nothing like her own: tired, looking past her reflection into the space beyond. That was another world, all mirrors were. A reflection but a creation, a different place that only seemed like this place when you looked at it, when you thought you knew it. Like her eyes. She thought she knew them but now they seemed more grey than green and the shadows beneath them belonged not on her face but on her dad's; those depths of worry he had put there. She brought a hand to the mirror and touched finger to finger. Her hand didn't pass through; she knew it wouldn't. There was only glass, cold and wet with steam. She held her hand there and thought of the Pale Fox, how it could pass between worlds, how if it was one day tired of its world it could simply leave it, pass through a mirror and begin again – for a while at least.

"That would be nice," she said and let her hand fall away.

When she was dressed in jeans and Skan's old *Avengers* T-shirt with the oversized fair isle jumper on top, her walking boots laced up tightly, she came downstairs to find her dad waiting for her, tapping his car keys against one hand as he leaned against the living room doorway watching the news. When he heard the stairs creak, he turned and looked her over.

"Why do you have to go into town anyway? Have you seen how it is out?" he asked, his voice full of the same worry she had seen in the mirror.

She wanted to tell him it didn't matter what she did, not if he was right. I'm going to see Isaac, she wanted to tell him, shout at him, and what does that matter if all this is ending?

Instead she said, coldly, "I told you, I want to go up the hill to the ruins." "Wouldn't you want me with you? There's a bad storm coming in later."

She paused, her hand lingering over her coat, and looked to him. "A real one?"

He was focused on the television, the news. "What do you mean?" he said, distracted by whatever was being said. "Of course a real one, worse than what's out there now."

She put on her duffel and checked her hair in the hall mirror, pushing stray strands to the sides. "I just want to do something by myself for a bit, take some pictures and stuff. Why's that a problem?"

"Okay, but listen, I want you back here by five. It's important, do you understand? You have to be home early, promise me you'll do that for me, Kyle."

She nodded. "I told you didn't I, I'm only going up the hill. I won't be long, I promise."

Promises, maybe it was a family trait that she seemed unable to keep one. *I promise.* It was all just words, not even written just spoken, temporary and fleeting, as weak as that.

He huffed and threw his keys in the air, caught them. "Let's get gone, then."

The world outside was white again. Not snow, but fog. It had rolled its way across all of Selny through the morning hours, ghosting the island into a veiled place of what might be hidden within the mist, and the white of it, a dirty white, swallowed up everything it crept over. Now it was low, clinging close to the

ground and making half the world unseen and the rest
seem like ships rising, fleetingly and in the knowledge
that they would sink again into the sea of mist.

There was a familiar silence between them as
they drove towards St Christopher; her dad tapping
his fingers without rhythm on the steering wheel,
nervous, lost in his own thoughts again. She knew she
should put her hand on his, stop it tapping, tell him it
was all alright, that he needn't worry. But instead she
looked out of her window and watched the moors, the
horses and the shafts of sunlight finding a way through
the cloud and darting down at the fogbound land.
As they came into town he started to hum, the tune
familiar to her.

"What is that?" she asked, still watching the
world rather than turning to see him. She could hear
the tap of his fingers on the staring wheel beneath
the hum.

"*The Only Living Boy In New York*. I used to play
it all the time for you when you couldn't sleep.
Once when you were teething I put you and Skan
in the car and drove all the way to Frodsham and
back. The only time you stopped crying was when
I played that, so I just kept playing it on repeat and
humming along. Poor Skan kept waking up and
asking me to turn it lower but I couldn't because it
was soothing you."

She said nothing. She thought of the girl, the angry words and how far away Skan was. Too far away to believe he might ever hear the same sonic boom.

By the time they reached the quayside, the world was already darkening, storm-heavy clouds stretching in all directions and ready to wake.

"You'll be soaked you know," he said as she got out. "Listen, why don't you just come home? Please, just for today."

Quickly, she pulled up her hood. "I told you, I'm fine." She slammed the door behind her. *I'll keep you safe*, she had promised but as the door hammered shut she knew that had been a hasty promise, one she could never have kept. *I'm sorry.* A weak whisper within her own head.

She hurried across the street to the ticket hut at the bottom of the hill where a girl her age was waiting to sell tickets for the funicular. There was no one else thinking of going up the hill today. She looked back and saw their car disappearing up and over the rise and out of town.

"Are you going up in this?" asked the ticket girl.

Kyle looked up. The funicular was old, the maroon paint flaking. There was a name painted on the side, the paint of that flaking too. *Hildebrand.* She wondered if that was the funicular's name or the company who once operated it. It would be nice if people named funiculars but she doubted they did. The hill was steep, the tracks lined either side with encroaching bushes before reaching a rocky stretch of the hill and then, after strain and pull, there was the flat summit and the broken-tooth remains of the church, that too lost in fog.

"I was going to," she said to the girl. The girl had blue hair and piercings, just like the girl in Skan's picture, but she was smiling. Kyle left her and ran through the fog down along the quayside, weaving between a group of local kids and then following the cobbled street around until she was at The Checky Cat. Isaac was standing outside, his hood up, looking down at his muddy boots. His rifle was wrapped and resting against the wall. His backpack was on the floor, empty and waiting to be filled.

She was out of breath by the time she reached him, slowing to a walk as he looked up. The necklace had leapt out from the cover of her jumper as she ran so she quickly tucked the silver owl back in, hiding it. She swallowed and took another glance back. *It's not too late, I could go back and pretend I can help him.* No, that was a lie. The truth was she only hoped for what she saw, an empty street and the fog now building like a living thing again along the quay.

"You're early," Isaac said, lifting his backpack. He

hefted it on to his shoulder and grabbed his rifle. "I didn't think you'd come, if I'm honest like."

"I said maybe didn't I?"

For a moment they stood there outside The Checky Cat, looking at each other, smiles as awkward and nervous as the silence between them, the gap waiting to be filled by whoever was braver. It was Isaac, it was always bound to be Isaac.

"There'll be no buses today," he said, standing taller as if doing that, making himself bigger than he already was would give him that boost of confidence. It seemed to work. "Not like this, be here all day this fog. It'll be walking for us if you can handle it."

She was still breathing hard, her chest burning. "My dad said it's going to rain. I don't mind the rain too much."

Isaac laughed. "It's not the rain but the mud that'll get you down. The moors will be a mess from last night and this morning, proper swampy. I listened to the weather alright, it's reckoned there'll be more rain today but if we start off now we might reach the stones before the whole moor's just one big bog. You ready?"

Again she glanced back. Again she saw the empty road, the quay, the waiting fishing boats, the lengthening and thickening fog rolling in from the sea.

"Did you bring anything to drink?" she said, realising all she had in her pockets were her cigarettes and phone.

Isaac tapped his backpack. "If you mean water I've got a bottle," he said, his teeth chalk-white as he smiled. "But if you mean something stronger, I've that too. Come on."

She let him pass her. She stood there, hands deep in her pockets, hesitating. She could hear herself breathing, heavy, fearful. Within the beat of it she could almost hear the woman's, her mother's, denial. *I think you've got the wrong number. Goodbye.*

"You coming?" he said from behind her.

She shook herself away from the memory and turned, pulled her hands out of her pockets bringing out her cigarettes. She gave a small smile and he smiled back. "I'm coming," she said as she lit a cigarette. She offered him one.

"Not likely. Those things'll kill you before life's done with you, that's what my dad always said and he should've known, it was them what killed him."

"Oh, that's awful, do you want me to…" she said, motioning to drop the cigarette.

He shrugged. "Not my place. Best we get going though, don't want to get stuck out there in this."

She took a quick drag and then threw the cigarette into a puddle where it sizzled and sank quickly. He was walking again, walking fast enough that she had to work to keep up with him, his backpack and the rifle now slung on his shoulder, making him look like a soldier on exercises. His eyes were set to the distance, sure to get there.

The fog cleared up a little as they followed the north road, but once the road started winding into the moors, it was there again so that she could barely see a few feet ahead or around them.

He looked across to her. "You're scared."

It wasn't a question. She had her hands shoved deep in her pockets, turning her lighter around and around. She had thought she had hidden her fear but he was right, she felt like she was in an old horror movie, that any minute there would be a howling from the moors.

"I've never walked in fog like this."

"Me neither, much. But I know the way blind. We always get this fog, thick like this coming off the sea and putting itself all about. My granddad used to call it the Kayo like it were alive and deserved a name but it's just fog, isn't it? Nothing to fear in fog."

"Apart from being out alone in it with a stranger," she said, looking up at him. He seemed taller, bigger too, like a giant leading her towards the hidden world of giants.

He laughed at that. "Nah, you've nothing to fear

there either. I'm not a stranger; you know my name and where I live. I gave you a present didn't I?"

"Present?" she said.

"The book." He looked at her, still both of them walking on through the fog, the Kayo. It was dark now too, the day giving up on itself early as the weather set in and the night impatiently followed. Grey: all the island was grey and dark. She swallowed. Yes, she was scared.

Before she could answer, her foot slipped, her ankle turning, mud sliding along her sole, and her body fell forward too quickly to stop herself. She cried out but she didn't hit the ground. Instead she felt Isaac's arm grab hers, pulling her up and back towards him and the force and momentum of the fall, the sudden grabbing of her arm, pulled her body into his, the two striking and joining so that the full weight of him hit her. She gasped, the cold air rushed into her lungs and with it the smell of him too. No aftershave or deodorant, just the smell of him, his sweat and his skin. Her head was against his jacket as she steadied herself.

"You alright?" he said, not letting go, and she looked up. His face was so close to hers. It made her want to look away, having someone's face so close.

She stepped back and he let go. "I think so, thank you."

He pushed his hair back from his face. "Can't imagine you would've broke much but best to be safe. As long as you're well."

"Yes, I'm fine. Thank you." She knelt down and touched her ankle. It was a little sore, that was all.

"Can you walk?" he said from way above her.

She looked up. His brow was set, worried for her. He looked like a bear, huge and strong, wild. "I think so, really you don't have to worry. I'll be fine if you give me a minute."

She made herself stand but his hand went to her arm again. Instinctively she pulled hers away, a little too quickly, and saw his face fall into confusion. "I'll be good, really I will," she said, taking a step or two forward, then turning around in a circle, exaggerating the movement. "See, I'm fine."

He made a grunt. More of the bear in him, still frowning, always frowning. Still hurt a little too.

"It's not far anyway now," he said and began to walk again.

She followed him, struggling now to keep up, not because of her ankle but because he walked so relentlessly. They left the road and followed a hard track east for a while where the track became stony and he told her to watch herself so she did, picking her way through the rocks, following his every step and turn. The fog was low to the ground now and she realised they were higher up. Her chest told her that too, tight and in need of a place to rest and find breath. But Isaac kept going.

"Did you read it then?" he said.

She wiped her brow, heavy with sweat. "A little. I mean I looked at it, you know, a few pages. It's sad isn't it, I mean I didn't think it would be sad but it seems just sad."

At last he stopped and putting his hands on his hips he rested, his broad chest rising and falling. "Sad. Yeah, if you like, maybe. Why though?"

He took out some water from his backpack and took a long drink then held it out to her. She took it and drank, trying not to think that his lips had been on it, that he had drunk from it. He watched her too as she drank, watched her as he had in the pub. Watched her like she was water and he wanted her to quench his thirst, all of her. When she had drunk she handed him the bottle back. They were quite high up and now the fog was low, she could see the sun setting, just a blush of orange below the clouds to the west. It wasn't late, not much past four, but it seemed to her that they had walked deep into the night and it dawned on her too that soon it would be true night and she would be alone with him, out here.

"Well," he said. "Come on with you. What made it sad then?"

She thought of the girl, Astrid, being left in Marorn without anyone. She thought of poor Jonas, alone in the field in Germany. She even thought of Kevarl, dying in the forest with everything he had wanted lost.

"It's lonely," she said at last. "I mean it seems that anyway."

He sighed, drank the rest of the water. "And what's wrong with loneliness? Plenty of people are lonely; if you ask me it's good that a book tells that sort of story. Look there."

He pointed with the water bottle across the moorland. She looked to where he was pointing and there, hovering over the moor, was the black shape of a hawk.

"Wouldn't say a hawk was lonely, not me. Look at it. It's alone isn't it but it's got happiness in that. Being alone doesn't mean you're lonely, sometimes being alone is just the way it is and for the best. Anyway, no one ends up alone in the book, not really, not even Jonas. You'll know that when you read it proper. If you ask me, he's with the Pale Fox wherever he goes. Being alone doesn't mean you're lonely, that's what I reckon anyway. I'd say you can be lonely when you're surrounded by a thousand friends. Nah, there's nothing lonely about any of it. Sad maybe, not lonely though."

He pushed the empty bottle back into the backpack, fumbling a little as he did. Now she could see it, why he loved the book. It was that loneliness. She had never realised it before but there was a loneliness to him, his too-small coat, his out-of-fashion and ill-fitting jeans and his clumsily waxed hair. Or at least, if not loneliness, he was used to being alone no matter how brash he came across, how rough his words were. Maybe that: his voice, his words, were part of it.

"There's nothing wrong with it, I suppose," she said, smiling at him. "I just thought it was sad, that's all."

"I get that but in the end they save the world, don't they?" he said, like he couldn't grasp at the sadness she saw, couldn't fathom it.

She thought of home and her friends and she thought of how they were the only two on the moor now, the only two for miles around. She thought of her dad, alone both within and without. 'What if the world ends?' she asked, uncertain she wanted to know his answer. "Would a person be lonely then?"

"Depends," he said, not turning to her. "If you were left with someone to be with then you wouldn't be lonely, would you? Like if the world ended right here and now and there was just you and me, I wouldn't be lonely. Would you?"

Her cheeks grew warm. "No. I don't think I would."

He scratched at his hair. "Anyway, there's not just here, is there? There being another world, a place that's safe and good, that's hardly sad is it? That's what Marorn is, it's different than here. It's a good place. I reckon what makes a book sad is them who read it, like if you want to feel sad about what happens then you can feel sad, but I don't ever feel sad, not about any of it. I don't think I could ever feel sad about there being another place besides all this." For a moment he looked off to the west, to the fast-diminishing light there, and then he looked back to her and smiled awkwardly, sadly. "We best keep going. The stones are just up that way, plenty of rabbits too. You can help me nab one if you like."

She should have felt sick at the idea. She knew that. If anyone back home had suggested shooting rabbits, the idea would never have pulled on her, made her so curious. But now it did, made her answer too quickly. "Yes, I'll help you."

They walked a little way further onto the moors, her boots sinking deeper into the mud with every step, the ground growing more rain-ruined and treacherous. It slowed them but eventually they reached the stones.

The Penny Stones were hardly Stonehenge, that

was her first thought. Not a tight circle of touching stones, no lintel stones to pull them together. These were widely spaced and jagged, each tip looking like it had been sliced off at an angle, huge knives, great axe heads. They were thin too. Not squat as she had imagined but tall, widening at the top but thin when seen from the side so she wondered why they hadn't toppled yet in the fierce island winds. In the middle of the widely spaced circle was a stone more like those she had expected. She knew what it was. It was more of an altar than a standing stone, one large and fat stone at the bottom with a long slab placed over it. It was half the height of the others but even from beyond the circle she could see the deeply gouged and scraped marks of the runes her dad had told her about. Scars all across a long dead body.

"Is that the Sun Stone?" she asked. "The one in the book?"

He let his backpack and rifle drop and gave a sigh, worked his shoulders. "That's it. Gateway to Marorn." He smiled at that so she wasn't sure if he was being serious or if he was making fun of himself, of what he believed.

The fog seemed to cling about the circle, wreathing it but not entering past the outer circumference.

"That's strange," she said. "The fog."

He nodded, kneeling and undoing his backpack,

taking out a bottle of brownish liquid, rum she guessed. "Didn't I tell you? Even the fog doesn't fancy going through to the other side." He unscrewed the top and took a long swig of the rum. He didn't flinch at the alcohol, just swallowed it down like it was lemonade, then handed it to her. She hesitated but then the cold hit her and she shivered, taking the bottle and bringing it slowly to her lips, hesitating before she drank.

"It won't kill you."

"I know." She drank it. It wasn't as warm as the whisky her dad bought, smoother; it didn't burn going down her throat and when it reached her stomach she felt warmer, better, and took another drink, longer this time.

"See," he said.

She handed it back. Isaac took a blanket from the backpack and throwing it out in one quick motion he rolled it over the grass.

He lowered himself onto the blanket, lying flat across it though his body was too long and his boots touched mud. Next he took the rifle, slid the covering away, then looked at her. "You going to stay there all day?"

There was little room left on the blanket. She would be close to him, their bodies touching.

"What for?" she asked and for an answer he put his

hand in his pocket and brought out his torch, flicked it on and shone it at her so the brightness, sudden and harsh, made her shield her eyes.

"Rabbits," he said.

She looked around. There were no rabbits, just the fog and the stones, but she was cold and the air seemed wet, like rain was nearing. She crossed the grass and lay down beside him, trying without success to keep a space between them. It was no good. Her coat touched his coat. His arm touched her arm. He was looking forward, north of the stones, not looking at her, just staring intently at the fog.

"There aren't any," she said.

"Shush," he answered, pointing with the lightless torch. "There."

She saw the fog and only the fog for a moment but then there was a shape moving slowly free of the fog, a greyish smudge. Or pale, she thought, pale within pale.

The shape hopped closer and passing out of the fog, she saw it clearly and with some disappointment, as just a rabbit. It looked this way then that, low to the grass, sniffing.

"Watch," he whispered. Quietly he brought the rifle up and placed the torch close to the sight. He lined the rifle and torch up with the rabbit then, against all reason of his bulk and awkwardness like

160

this was the one thing his body knew to do with slightness, with ease, he deftly flicked the torch on so the light shone like a bullet at the rabbit. Immediately its sniffing and fidgeting ceased and it was held there, still as the stones. Isaac moved a little closer to her. She watched his finger on the trigger and then looked to the rabbit and back to the trigger. She knew what was coming. Her breath quietened but she could feel her heart beating. Racing fast. Though he was so close to her, she couldn't feel his heart beating. Calmly, he squeezed the trigger. There was a horrible crack but the rabbit made no sound, just flopped to the side. Isaac turned on to his side. She saw the delight on his face.

"Easy as that," he said and he laid the rifle on the blanket between them. "What do you reckon?"

"Reckon?" She had reckoned she should have screamed at seeing him shoot the rabbit or at least felt sick. But there had been nothing. Just the crack and the rabbit falling, no pang of emotion, no sense of the unfairness of the whole thing, no loss. Just a crack.

"Could you shoot one?"

She looked at the rifle and her hand reached for it. It was light, not a heavy and cruel thing, just wood and metal. "I think so."

He moved close to her again, his whole body

pressing against her now. "Good. Now hold it out like I did." She held the rifle as he did, the butt along the line of her shoulder.

"Not quite," he said and without asking her permission his hands were on hers, readjusting her, making subtle changes in how she held it until he was satisfied.

"That's it, now it'll jerk but if you keep a tight hold you'll be good. I'll shine the torch and when you've got it sighted, you can shoot when you're ready. You ready?"

She nodded. She looked along the sight. There were no rabbits and part of her hoped the crack of the first shot might have scared them away. For a time that seemed to stretch and linger there was only the fog but then, a mixture of thrill and fear in her, she saw the faint shape moving closer.

"It's the grass," he whispered. "They like the grass around the stones."

"What grass is it?" she asked, focused on the shape as it left the fog's safety. She felt his body shrug. "Just grass I'd say, rabbit grass."

She smiled. He lifted the torch. "Ready," he whispered and the sun-bright torch shone at the rabbit. Frozen, it stared back into the light. She expected her hands to tremble a little, to become unsteady with what she was about to do, but she was as calm as Isaac had been. No racing heart, just certainty.

She squeezed the trigger. Then there was the crack and leap, her arm jerking. This time there was no lie of silence. The rabbit made a squeaking scream that turned her stomach. Now her heart raced once more. The rabbit screamed again, so small and desperate. She let the rifle fall and followed the light of Isaac's torch to see it lying there, jerking, its tiny body in spasm, a fleck of red on its side.

"Almost," said Isaac flatly as he stood. "You'll get one clean next time."

She couldn't move. She could only watch the rabbit, legs kicking and head shaking as if it was saying *no, I don't want this, no*. But Isaac was on it quickly, long strides crossing the space between the stones and rabbit in no time. Without hesitation he knelt down and picked it up. She almost called out to him to stop but instead she lay there and watched as he took the rabbit's body in one strong hand so it finally stopped jerking and his other great hand gripped the neck. There was another crack, quieter this time but more complete in its purpose. He held the rabbit by its ears, and found the first, brought them both back to the blanket and shoved them roughly into his backpack. She stood and waited for him to finish.

She hadn't felt the tears on her cheeks but when he was done he looked at her and his hand touched her cheek. She jerked away a little but when his finger touched her she felt the wetness of her tears. "You been crying?" he said, almost confused by the sight of tears. "Nothing to cry over you know. They're just rabbits."

"It's not that," she lied.

He stepped closer. He was a stone, tall and solid, the scar on his cheek his own unknowable rune. She knew what he was going to do and the thought wasn't so repulsive. If she was honest, she would have preferred it to have been Spencer stood there, moving his body closer to hers, watching him consider how to kiss her, but it was Isaac and she didn't hate the idea of that.

She lifted her head and saw him looking down at her, crystal-blue eyes a contrast to the roughness of him.

"I'm okay, really," she managed to say.

His hand held her arm, wrapped tightly around it easily. *It's okay*, she wanted to say, *I want this too*. She could see him doubting himself so she closed her eyes and brought her lips to his and as they kissed his hand gripped her arm firmer, holding her to him. His kiss was hard as she knew it would be, but wet, too wet. His tongue touched her tongue and she felt his other hand push into her coat and slip beneath her jumper. His cold hand against her stomach made her jump but she didn't push him away. Time and the world were far away. The wetness of his lips was strange but she liked how their teeth clacked and their tongues touched and she liked how she felt safe against him. But soon his hand began to move higher, from her stomach to her bra.

"Wait," she said, breaking the kiss. But he didn't wait. He pulled her close to him again and he kissed harder. His hand was beneath her bra now, gripping her, pawing her, and she could feel how much he wanted more than this and she knew she didn't. At first, yes, she had wanted to kiss him but now she knew that none of this was for her. It was all for him and she had only let it happen because she had lied to herself that she wanted it too. But not this. Not here. Not with him. She pulled his hand from her breast and turned her head away, saliva trailing from their parting lips. But still he didn't let go of her arm. She struggled, tried to pry his fingers away but he was too strong and his other hand reached out and grabbed her jumper.

"Isaac!" she shouted but he didn't answer, his head moving towards her again to kiss. "No!" she shouted and she hit his chest as hard as she could. Now he let go but as he did she felt her mother's necklace cold against her neck and though she didn't hear it break, she felt the pull of it and the sudden release as Isaac kept hold of it, breaking the links at the back of her neck. She pushed him away as hard as she could but only managed to make herself fall back onto the blanket. His eyes were glassy, like he wasn't there. He rubbed his face and only then did he seem to see her on the floor.

"I'm sorry," he said, the necklace still in his hand. "I thought…"

He moved to help her stand but she hit his hand away. Now she knew she was crying, her eyes streaming but not out of fear or loss. She hit his hand again and then she brought it hard across his face, an echo of the rifle's crack. Numb, he shook his head.

"I said sorry didn't I," he said.

"I'm fifteen," she screamed at him. "I'm fifteen!"

"I didn't mean to," he said, stumbling over his words. "Kyle…I wasn't go to…I wouldn't have…"

"You would!" she shouted and she lashed out, her nails scraping against his neck. "You would, you know you would!"

She heard him say her name but she didn't wait to hear anything more. Turning, she ran, his stupid calls fading behind her as she ran harder and harder so the fog took her and though she couldn't see where she was going she kept running. It was raining, the mud trying its best to pull her down though nothing could stop her from getting far away from Isaac, from the stones. She was crying, the rain washing the tears away only for more to come. She could still taste him, his lips, his tongue. She could still feel him, the remnant mark of his hands as if they were still holding her, gripping her. She ran and ran and when at last she stopped she knew she was lost.

"Kyle," came a distant call. She turned to where she thought it came from and it came again. A strange bird calling to its mate. "Kyle!" Yet now it seemed to come from a different direction. Turning, turning, the sound seemed to come from everywhere around here and nowhere, so faint now it seemed not of this place but of elsewhere or of her mind. The fog was fast dispersing, the rain chasing it away. She could see the moors though they were merely a lesser dark against the night. No stones. No road. No Isaac. "Kyle!" he called again but this time it seemed even further away, a world away.

There came a deep rumbling that at first she took for thunder but then as she stood there, uncertain of which way to go, what way to run to take her home, she felt the rumbling coming up through the muddy ground and before she could move, the horses were tearing past her. One after another they galloped by, so close she could feel their heat and smell them, water spraying from their flanks and onto her face as they raced past. She didn't move. She was a stone. She was a circle of her own making, just her body alone, deep-rooted in the ground so that nothing could ever, would ever, move her. No stranger's hand. No familiar hand. No one. She closed her eyes and waited to be struck but the rumbling calmed and the heat of the horses' bodies soon passed and she was alone.

Chapter Ten

Rose Cottage wasn't home, not truly, but as she
followed the road up from the big house to the little
cottage, wet through and raw-eyed, she felt the same
relief as if it had been her home, the home she had
always known. She was exhausted, her legs heavy
and her boots thickly caked with mud. Her duffel felt
like a suit of cumbersome armour, so waterlogged,
and the rain had managed to find its way through her
T-shirt to her skin, so she shivered uncontrollably
as she walked the final few yards to the green door.
She almost called out for her dad but she was too
tired even for that. Her head low, her hair a mess and
clinging damply to her head, she saw the painted rose.
Dirty raindrops smeared its petals and looking up she
saw the gutter was full, dammed up with the flood,
and overflowing; clay-brown water dripping down

the wall onto the little ceramic tile. She pulled her jumper's sleeve down over her hand and wiped the tile clean but even as she pulled her hand away, the gutter water dripped down and discoloured the tile once again.

The front door wasn't locked. She was glad of that. Glad she didn't have to knock only for him to see how she was and ask why she was how she was. She had no words. She wanted no words. All she wanted was to lie on her bed and stop. To forget. Not forever, not to give up. Just to stop for a while until her mechanisms, her workings that were so tired out and broken, found the strength to begin again. *I don't care how long that takes.* She pushed the door open and stepped inside. *I could stop for a year if it meant I could start again.*

The house was quiet and there were no lights on anywhere. The storm her dad had promised was truly building now so the wind battered the cottage, catching the door behind her and slamming it shut with a sudden finality. The pitch black within was momentarily lit up by a flash of light outside that was followed by the cleaving crash of thunder. She took off her coat and jumper, threw them over the banister only for the coat to fall in a heap to the floor. Still she shivered. Her T-shirt clung to her and now the lack of constant soaking made her feel oddly hot, sick as if she was sweating with a fever. She didn't go upstairs straight away. Instead she moved drowsily to the living room. He was there, sitting on the floor with a glass in his hand. The television was on the floor too, toppled on its side, and there was a smell of smoke, of burning, which she saw came from a heap of ashes in the middle of the carpet, a black circle burnt through to the floorboards below.

"Dad," she said, folding her arms about her body to try to stop the shivering.

He lifted his head as if just woken from a deep sleep and turned to look at her. His eyes were as raw as hers but he looked at her like he was struggling to remember who she was, those raw eyes scrunching up to black dots.

"Kyle," he said, a weak smile, and he waved an arm towards the television. Whisky sloshed from his glass. "The electricity went out. Bound to, I suppose."

Another flash, much brighter this time and then the booming to follow. He jumped a little and when it had passed he drank the whisky.

"You're wet," he said. "Come sit with me."

She didn't want to. She wanted her room, her bed, her own empty part of the world. That hollow in the universe that always seemed unreachable. But she found herself crossing the room and letting her body drop down beside him. She rested her head on his shoulder and closed her eyes. *Maybe, I can sleep here. Maybe.*

"Do when I took you and Skan to Edinburgh Zoo?" said her dad, disturbing her promised sleep. She said nothing. Let her mind wander. She had no memory of a zoo or Edinburgh but his voice was soft and familiar and she stayed there, letting him speak. "I don't know why but I started thinking about that day, couldn't stop once I'd started. They had lemurs there, do you remember, but the thing was you went into this sort of enclosure and the lemurs were loose. We went in together, the three of us. It was like a jungle, wild almost. You grabbed my hand right from the start but Skan didn't, he started walking ahead calling out for the lemurs but then they were there, two of them, running at us out of nowhere and Skan started screaming and you started crying so I had to scoop you both up, even Skan, and go back out the way we came in. Do you remember that?"

"Yes," she said. Maybe she would dream it, maybe if she dreamed it, she could remember the dream from now on.

Light cut through the darkness. The hammer of thunder stole the silence away.

He laughed. "I brought you here to be safe." He laughed again and stroked her hair, his hand unsteady. "Safe. How did I ever believe that?"

She felt him sobbing before she heard him. His body jerking against her. She thought of the rabbit, jerking then still forever. His sobs grew louder and louder. "Safe," he kept saying through the tears. "Safe."

She opened her eyes. "You didn't bring *me* here, Dad," she said, standing so his sobbing body collapsed onto his side and he lay there crying on the carpet. "I brought *you* here to save you."

He was curled up into a ball now, body rocking on its side. She saw a broken glass beside the ashes. *That's him, broken into too many pieces to mend.* No glue would ever stick.

"You don't understand," he said, still rocking, still crying. "This is it, Kyle. This is the day the world ends but look at it, it's just a day, just another day."

She stepped back towards the door. He looked like a child crying for a toy he had been told he couldn't have. He was worse than broken; he was shattered and gone. She shook her head. This wasn't how it was meant to be, she knew that, a father wasn't meant to do this, not ever. They were meant to protect you, not drag you into their own little ending, their sundering. And now it hit her and wouldn't let her go, that devastating realisation. She hated him. She hated him more than she hated anyone, more than she hated Isaac or the idea of the world ending or her

Mum for leaving or Skan for living a life. She hated him because all of it, this, now, everything, was his fault and always had been. She began to shake again, not with the cold or the rain or fear but with a rage that didn't want to leave her, a rage she didn't want to let go of.

"No!" she screamed as the lightning flashed. "No!" Her cry vied with the thunder. He stopped rocking and scrambled up onto his knees, wild-eyed.

"No!" she shouted, louder, full of fury. "It's not ending. Nothing is ending. The world won't ever end, Dad, it's stronger than that. It doesn't break just like that, just because you think it will. You're the only one who breaks. You break everything. You broke Mum, you broke Skan, you broke everything... you broke us!"

She reached out for anything and found the remote, hurling it at him with all her strength. She didn't care whether it struck him. She didn't stay to see or give him a chance to speak. She hurried into the hall and threw the door open. Out, she ran once more into the rain. It was almost a relief to feel it cover her again, wash away the burning anger that had filled her, cool her and calm her. She didn't care that she didn't have her coat. She didn't care if she froze, if it killed her. She ran through it, down the sloping road towards the big house as the lightning lit the darkness and the thunder was like a constant drum, beating for her, calling her on.

Outside the big house Isaac stood in the middle of the road with his arms out, his body open but his fists clenched, wrought with tension. He looked like the painting of Jesus, not giving forgiveness but asking for it, and yet his great frame standing in the road was more of a barrier than an apology.

"Where are you going in this?" he called. He was as soaked as her, but he stood there like the rain didn't exist, like it wasn't running in rivers down his jacket, down his face.

"Away," she said and she walked to her right, towards the cliffs and away from the road.

"Wait," he said and he opened one fist. The necklace was there.

"I don't want it!" she shouted over a boom that came without the warning of light.

He frowned and closed his hand around the necklace again, concealing it almost in shame. "I'm sorry."

"At least you say it," she called and his mouth moved to speak but no words came. She kept walking, leaving the smooth road for the boggy grass of the moor.

"Kyle," he called but she didn't turn back. "Be careful. The horses, they don't like thunder much."

She walked harder. When she felt she was far enough away from the road she looked back, thinking that he must be following her but instead she saw him standing in the exact place where she had left him, solitary and unmoving.

The moors rose towards the cliffs. There was an old dirt path that ran south to join up with the ramblers' paths that skirted the cliffs all the way back east towards St. Christopher. Eventually the moorlands became scrubland and she could hear the sea, angry waves attacking the cliffs, relentless and stubborn in their assault. Together with the booming thunder and near-biblical downpour, the world was full of angry sounds. She wanted to join in, scream out as she walked, let every last drop of the held-in out, but instead she walked in silence and as she walked she took out her phone. She went to Spencer's last message, saw his black-and-white selfie, a water tower at his back. She typed "I'll be home next week" and pressed send though she could see there was no signal. The message, though written, floated there in between the time of sending and receiving, of saying and hearing. A frozen voice but a voice at least. She smiled and put her phone away, breathing in the rain-freshened air, her lungs gratefully sucking in the night's almost heady oxygen.

There was a sound and she turned to it. She half-expected to see a faint shape, a flash of white passing, returning, but there was only the dark and the rumbling sound. No ghost. No fox passing between the worlds. Once was enough, to see it and know it. Once was all that was needed.

The rumbling was not thunder. She knew that even as she stopped and listened to it. It came from the moor, close by, and she knew she should move quickly. Get away from it. But instead she made herself wait and turned towards the oncoming beat of hooves, felt the sound move up her legs, gentle music, a steady beat. But even as she listened the sound seemed to change direction so that now it came from her right. She turned again and again it shifted. Now it was behind her. Maybe the horses were not near. Maybe the sound came from somewhere else, from another world. Maybe the horses would pass right by her and she wouldn't even see them, phantoms beyond her reach, their Riders seeing her as a ghost. She held out a hand, reaching out, trying to find a way into that other world but there was only rain and air and the ever-nearing rumble. A flash of immense brilliance filled the dark and turning to it she looked south to the cliffs and saw another and another and another flash. They seemed far away, much further than lightning ever was, and no sound followed. Just those distant flashes. England was that way, the world her dad had dreamt was ending was that way. She felt the ground beneath her begin to shake and knew now for certain that the horses were almost upon her. Calmly, she let her eyes close and imagined another world, not one far away or written of in a book. There was no fox in this world. No pale ghosts. It was a real world, one she could go to and be part of. She imagined her dad being there and her mum too, Skan, everyone. Her life was there too, waiting for her to live it. Not Marorn; it didn't need a name. It just was what it was: a good place, and a place she deserved to know. Not this place where everything was broken. She knew now that this breaking had been happening for years, around her and within her, without her and because of her, through her and beyond her. Cracking and shattering, slow fault lines spreading and widening until they fell apart and were truly broken forever. Her dad had been right. Worlds end and there is nothing a person can do to stop that. All people could do was hope there might be somewhere else where they could be safe and go there if they were lucky. She longed to be that lucky.

But for now there was only this. Kyle, alone on the moor not far from the island's edge, her eyes shut tight and the wild horses nearing though she would not step out of their path. *Let them, just let them. It could end like this.* No hand to crush. No weight bearing down. No sudden violence or flames consuming. No burning world. No hammer, just light. Just thunder in the night.